NADJA

THE LIBRARIAN'S HOPE

5. xii. 2024

To Liam. Who will note that while the story invokes the Three Furies, no mention is made of the Vatican or The Trinity

NADJA

THE LIBRARIAN'S HOPE

Gregory Andrusz

La Cage Imaginaire
Hampstead

Matador
Unit E2 Airfield Business Park,
Harrison Road, Market Harborough,
Leicestershire. LE16 7UL
Tel: 0116 279 2299
Email: books@troubador.co.uk
Web: www.troubador.co.uk/matador
Twitter: @matadorbooks

ISBN 978 1 80514 216 4

British Library Cataloguing in Publication Data.
A catalogue record for this book is available from the British Library.

Printed and bound by CPI Group (UK) Ltd, Croydon, CR0 4YY
Typeset in 11pt Aldine401 by Troubador Publishing Ltd, Leicester, UK

Matador is an imprint of Troubador Publishing Ltd

For
Ochi Chornye

PROLOGUE

Francesco Puccini, wearing loose-fitting, faded jeans and a white T-shirt emblazoned with the smiling face of Socrates, came out of the Montelorenzo post office. He walked a few metres before sitting down on the low balustraded parapet that formed part of the medieval wall surrounding the hilltop town. He slowly took out a pocketknife and carefully slit open the small package for which he had had to sign. Inside was a *memento mori* - which was, at the same time, a *memento vivere* – for which he had been waiting. A woman passing by turned her head and, for some reason or other known only to herself, assuming that he had received a present, wished him happy birthday. As his faint smile drifted after her, a tear curled up in the corner of one eye and grew in volume until a fine crack formed in the dam holding back his feelings and a rivulet trickled down the gully between his cheek and nose. He waited for the flow to stop, then, moistening his forefinger, wiped away the clammy stain and strolled towards his home.

Before Mussolini's Fascists came and drained the marshes, the land in this northern tip of the Maremma, between the sea and the mammillary honey-coloured Tuscan hills, had been a malarial plain. In the 1950s, Montecatini – one of Italy's largest industrial companies at the time – had planted in the middle of this now-fertile arable landscape a monstrous 140-metre-high chimney, banded in the colours of a barber's pole. Although the fertiliser factory provided employment for several hundred people from the surrounding area, this Trajan column – a celebratory symbol of the triumph of industrial modernity over rural backwardness – was regarded by locals and visitors alike as a hideous eyesore.

Today, the main arterial road, the ancient Roman highway from Rome to Genoa, the Via Aurelia, hugs the coast until Fortecantina, then bulges inland and runs across the plain past the disfiguring blot on the landscape towards Grosseto. Not far from the coast, a narrow tarmac road forks off this main highway and winds up and around a hill clad in olive and holm oak trees. It then runs along the base of a high medieval wall, on which Francesco Puccini had been sitting, until it reaches the Porta del Mare when the road becomes a triumphal Via Roma. After a hundred metres or so, it begins to narrow before petering out in Piazza Garibaldi, as does the winner in the annual ten-kilometre race, like a Pheidippides or, less dramatically, like Joris and Dirck bringing the good news from Ghent to Aix.

An imposing yellow building belonging to the languid *carabinieri*, the guardians of a noisy Italian peace, sits on the final bend. Almost opposite this commanding edifice, once the grand villa of a wealthy Pisan family, is Il Cinghiale Bianco, an expensive restaurant of provincial fame which, despite its location, still feels the need to be protected by prowling Alsatian dogs. It's at this point that a smaller road sneaks off to the right and initially takes the visitor away from the town before spiralling up and around the hill to a scrap of land where cars park. A gravel path in one corner leads up to the ruins of a castle, attached to the wall of which is a recently repainted wooden noticeboard informing the visitor that this is a *Medieval castle built between the tenth and fifteenth centuries on the remains of an Etruscan fortress dating from the end of the fourth century BC*.

★

Every night, some three thousand Tuscan souls, one-fifth over the age of seventy, many with hands as gnarled as the olive trees they tend, close their shutters and go to bed. Their number has remained constant for decades, for not all those who are born and grow up there leave for ever; the caste-like structure reproduces its self-employed butcher and baker, carpenter and plumber, doctor, bar-owner and notary; its publicly covenanted road sweeper and postman; and its privately hired and fired construction worker. At night, they all slumber in the tightly packed houses below that symbol of feudal dominion, the castle, which despite its age will long outlast the hideous belching and polluting chimney of bourgeois power.

Ever since the sixties, the summer months have seen the local population swell as Lombards descend from the north, not as pillagers but as tourists, renting rooms in the town or erecting their tents on one of the two camping sites outside it. In more recent times, as Europeans have become richer, some of the visitors from near or abroad have bought and renovated run-down properties and metamorphosed into tax-paying, temporary residents. In doing so, these incomers, whether as renters or purchasers, have stimulated the building trade and breathed seasonal life into the local economy.

I used to visit Montelorenzo regularly, and each time I noticed how a little more of the castle keep had been restored, and how the town's ramparts had grown in jagged height. The cleverly engineered restoration was confined to tidying up the ruins just enough to satisfy the yearning of today's peregrinators to taste and savour, in person, the authentically medieval. Having seen, touched and supped in the past, they are free to concoct a vision of the past as they would like to imagine and remember it.

While traipsing about these ruins and restorations, some visitors occasionally experience a vague metaphysical pleasure – in much the same way as did pilgrims when visiting holy shrines – others serve the mundane purpose of providing a source of income for the locals, who stare down at them from their shuttered windows like weatherworn gargoyles.

⋆

A small, polished brass plate on the wall of a three-storey house (No. 6) on Piazza Garibaldi tells the world that this is where Alessandro Galgano lives. Another plaque, more prominently placed and cemented into the wall on the other side of the main entrance, bears the words *In memory of the men and women who died fighting for the fatherland between 1935 and 1945*.

It also tells anyone who might bother to read the inscription that it was placed there by none other than A. Galgano, a scion of a long-standing Montelorenzo family. Although it does not say so, one of his nineteenth-century ancestors had been introduced to Elisa Bonaparte during her visit to this small hilltop town soon after her brother, none other than Napoleon, had appointed her Grand Duchess of Tuscany. This happened about three years before he was exiled to the island of Elba, which I can see from where I am sitting and recalling the local legend that follows.

It's a tale that has taken me a short lifetime to put together. Making sense of all my notes has not been easy. But though it's been a task that has sapped my energy and diverted me from doing other things, every now and then I've glimpsed from the corner of my eye, like one does shooting stars on clear nights, the faces of those who, in chance conversations over the years, have added a touch of colour or detail to my own image of Montelorenzo as a Bosch-like canvas of The Garden of Earthly Delights. These (usually diurnal) flashes convinced me that since the story has acquired legendary status, it deserves recording.

⋆

When much younger, long before I knew him, Alessandro Galgano had once poetically described Montelorenzo as 'that little town smelling of scorched cork… where in the faces of its inhabitants one can read the desire for a lost peace'. Following the premature death of his parents, the would-be poet was forced to lower himself down like a Raphaelian *putto* from a drifting carpet of clouds to earn a living. This he did by opening a campsite, whose clientele he imagined would consist of predominantly lower-middle-class Italians searching for a modestly priced holiday away from the multitudes, who descend to the seaside in August for the *ferie estive*.

His campsite, which lay below the town on a fold in the castle-topped hill, was spread out over a series of terraces that were divided up into plots, each with its own olive tree and space for a car and a tent. In the evening, these latest invaders from the north, their sun-dried skins freshly caressed with oily fragrances following hours basking in a cloudless sky, would look up to the town and prepare for an evening assault on its bars and restaurants.

By the time I was introduced to him, Alessandro had been widowed for several years and had sole responsibility for caring for his son and daughter. Although regarded as a 'good catch', no one had come forward to declare a willingness to share the joy and shoulder the burden of bringing up two adolescent children. Left alone to the task, he found it easier to concede to their teenage requests and to desist from exerting parental authority over their behaviour. Each summer, Annabelle, his genial daughter, a student of modern languages, spent a few weeks at the campsite, playing tennis on its court, swimming in its pool and, now and then, lending a courteous teenage hand to the running of the family business. Her studious, entrepreneurially oriented and ambitious younger brother spent most of his time reading and devising money-making schemes.

Now in his early fifties, portly but not overweight, bouncy and well preserved, Alessandro never disguised the high regard he felt for Costanza Veronese, an elegant pharmacist from Florence. She owned an early nineteenth-century two-storey farmhouse which had been stylishly renovated by her former lover, a golf-playing, fair-haired architect and the son of the local baker, whom she had met when they were both students in Bologna. Costanza's solitary retreat lay just outside and well below the town's encircling wall, separated from Signor Galgano's thriving campsite enterprise by a car-wide, uneven, stony dust track and, beyond that, by a grove of high-yielding, mature olive trees.

Like Alessandro Galgano, she also had a son and daughter, who were virtually the same age as his two children. On the face of it, the cultured Signora Veronese and the affable Signor Galgano made a good town-and-country match. However, from her side, two principal factors militated against their companionable relationship evolving into anything more intimate. One was that she was weary of being courted by suitors more than ten years her senior, and she saw no reason why, in her late thirties, she should hasten the transition from vivacious maturity to premature decline into tetchy old age. Her children constituted the other main obstacle. Still in their early teens, they were too possessive to find in themselves the reserves of generosity to allow their mother to sprinkle some of her abundance of human warmth and love on another person.

Despite having occasionally caught the sound of rattling bones in her sealed cupboards, Alessandro lacked the willpower to resist presenting himself as her unwavering admirer. She was equally consistent in her behaviour towards him, making it unflinchingly clear that her displays of amicability should never be misconstrued as affection. Moreover, she quickly doused any candle-flickering idea that she could hide behind a Venetian carnival mask and become party to a temporary *liaison dangereuse.* This left her shaking her head at the sad and sobering thought that intergenerational marriages, on the whole, tended to combine materially beneficial social security packages with emotional death warrants. Nevertheless, the fact that she kept house down there on the hillside and he kept house up there in the square did not deter her from turning to him when, on the odd occasion, she felt that he could help her navigate the town's subterranean whirlpools of petty intrigues and thereby resolve a minor but nonetheless vexing and seemingly interminable issue involving, say, a tradesman or local resident who had taken umbrage at something she had said or done (or not done).

★

As one of the self-styled patricians in the area, Alessandro had convinced himself that the town, with which his family had such strong personal connections, should have a library, a place where information on its history and local current affairs would be available to both the local inhabitants and visitors to the area. Who, he asked, would not be interested to know that in September 1849, just a month after Garibaldi's pregnant wife, the love of his life, had died, this notoriously womanising revolutionary had anchored in a cove not far from Montelorenzo? According to local folklore, just when the great man's whole world had collapsed and he feared being captured, his aides assured him that, because he and his cause had the full support of the people of this local town, whose ringing bells were within earshot, he was safe and should therefore relax.

Half a century after this event, the town decided to mark his brief stopover in the vicinity by renaming its tiny square in his honour, as happened throughout Italy, even in places to which he had never been remotely near. Not long afterwards, the council went one stage further and erected a statue depicting him in one of his characteristically triumphant poses. Both this folklore and Garibaldi's immortalisation in marble figured prominently in Alessandro Galgano's advocacy of the library. Despite his own political inclinations, he never missed a chance to applaud the local council for its promotion of the town's association with this colossus in modern Italian history.

He made every effort to persuade those with power and influence that having named the piazza after Giuseppe Garibaldi and called the main street Via Camillo Cavour, nothing could be better than to name the library in honour of Giuseppe Mazzini, thereby completing the town's tribute to the trinity behind Italian independence and unification. Since not even his most implacable enemies were able to counter his propaganda offensive in the council chamber, the necessary funds were found for this civic project. Alessandro's public celebration of the local authority's decision was modest and muted, in glaring contrast to the jubilant private banquet which he held at his house for a handful of relatives and close friends who understood the immense gratification he felt at achieving his ambition.

After years of standing derelict, the building between Casa Galgano and one of the two bars in the town was converted into a well-stocked municipal library, more or less on time and with only minor hiccups, one of the more salient of which was an unwise aside made by Fausto Puccini, the local architect. In an unguarded moment he had hinted, while in the company of a visiting journalist, that the building's modernist interior furnishing was strikingly evocative of Montecatini's pre-war headquarters in Milan that had been created for Guido Donegani, the company's then-president.

The slightest suggestion of such an association was sufficient to dribble a drop of substance onto the rumour that the company's present owners had contributed generously to the cost of the building's refurbishment. According to the tittle-tattlers, especially those with a predilection for conspiracy theories, should the story circulating prove to be even half true, everyone in the town should take it upon themselves to be a vigilant watchdog on the lookout for any sign whatsoever of the company's undisclosed intentions. In the eyes of two quite unconnected coteries, it went without saying that any act of munificence by this donor should be viewed with suspicion.

However, this time, the town council expressed no such qualms about whether or not the company (renamed Montedison following its merger with another large company) had any ulterior motive. Contrary to what would have been expected of a politically leftist town council, its approach had been startlingly pragmatic. A sub-committee had been set up under the mayor with the brief to seek sponsorship from other corporate bodies for what was being referred to as the 'library initiative'. The mayor's faith in the merits and timing of the project was rewarded.

Within months, he was able to announce that, through the intense campaign of his hard-working team, ample funding had been available to cover the library's capital and running costs. The well-publicised success of the 'library initiative' attracted further substantial donations from two philanthropic trusts. One was sufficient to cover the cost of stocking the library with a respectable collection of encyclopaedias and reference books. The other was used to underwrite the library's subscription to a range of popular magazines, a few more specialist periodicals and a selection of newspapers representing stables of opinion across the entropic Italian political spectrum. In order to fulfil its function as a modern public library, a trestle table at its entrance was stacked with expensively produced publicity leaflets, some of which had been rendered into grammatically faultless German and English, reflecting the importance attached by the *comune* to broadening the town's appeal to foreign tourists.

Prominently displayed on a shelf at eye level, next to a brand-new set of encyclopaedias, were two thick, burgundy-red, leather-bound copies of the official history of Montelorenzo and its surrounding area. These two sumptuously produced texts represented nothing less than Alessandro Galgano's impressive magnum opus, of which he was justly proud. The gold embossed lettering on their spines was calculated to catch the attention of the browsing visitor or anyone sitting on one of the comfortable, padded tubular metal chairs positioned around one of three black faux hide-covered tables.

★

The library opened daily (except on Sunday) at specified but irregularly kept times. Its bright space and relaxing atmosphere attracted individuals of every age, including a handful of young people, the would-be escapees from their physically confining and emotionally stifling birthplace. Largely because it met the non-material needs of a revolving group of not-to-be neglected users, this modest public building was, like San Stefano's church just a stone's throw away, never completely empty.

Alessandro Galgano's trump card in securing support for his project had been his proposal that Francesco Puccini should be appointed as the librarian. Since the law required the post to be publicly advertised, the number of candidates applying for the job was far greater than anticipated. Yet, even though two of the candidates from nearby towns had certificates of librarianship and a few years' experience of working in libraries, it was common knowledge that Franco was destined to be offered the job. No one doubted that since this was a cosy sinecure, he would find it difficult to decline the offer when it was made. Even the few critics who muttered disapproval of his appointment accepted that, although he lacked certain formal qualifications required for the post, his possession of a university degree in classics and philosophy meant that in educational terms he met the necessary requirements. Moreover, he was a familiar figure in the community, known for his affability and public spiritedness. On top of these merits, another major asset lay behind his selection to be the librarian: Franco came from what the ruling political party in the *comune* regarded as a 'good family' - one which had a secure place in the Montelorenzene pantheon of working-class heroes.

The elevation of the family's status had begun with the deeds and accomplishments of a nineteenth-century Puccini patriarch. Its social ranking had received a Big Bertha-like boost during the Second World War when Franco's uncle became the unofficial chairman of an underground liberation committee and took part in several daring – some said foolhardy – partisan raids. The roadside memorial stone erected at the site in the valley below the town, where he had been executed by German troops in 1944 consolidated the family's standing in the community. It also advanced the progress of the Puccini dynasty within the Italian Communist Party. The combination of the family's civic reputation and political party activism had, prior to Franco's appointment, seen the election of his elder brother, Antonio, to become the town's Communist mayor.

The long pendulum swing in favour of the Puccini family had been at the expense of the Galganos who, until the Italian government ceased to be Germany's wartime ally, had long been the local kingpins. These days, the only way in which Alessandro, the surviving senior Galgano in the area, could have any effective say in local matters was as an anonymous promoter of local projects. But, even then, any proposal that emanated from him – such as the library, which was his most notable to date – would only be adopted after it had been filtered through one or other municipal committee, normally dominated by the Puccini family, their friends or political associates. Even after having cleared this hurdle, his involvement had to remain peripheral and indirect. Because of the actual and perceived wounds that the inhabitants of this typical Italian hilltop polity had experienced over many years, some self-inflicted, his efforts never received the public acknowledgement that they deserved. As a result, he rarely enjoyed any kudos arising from a project's success, except sometimes when he received a condescending wink or pat on the back.

★

Dressed in a baby blue linen shirt and contrasting byzantine blue trousers, Franco was standing behind a large, cluttered desk flipping through an album of black and white photographs. Opposite him was a woman of advanced middle age in a conventional black dress with an unconventional orange-tinted fringe of hair. She was clutching a cordovan brown, brass-clasped handbag on her lap. From the expression on her face and the way she sat, an observer might have presumed that she was talking to a funeral director or, alternatively, to a less solemn – but equally obsequious – solicitor but not to a librarian, particularly this one, whose totally informal attire matched his unpretentious nature.

"That's the most extraordinary enquiry I've had for a long time," Franco said in his usual barely audible but Gatling gun speed monotone.

"It was Marina who suggested that I should come and ask your advice. She said that you might have some sort of catalogue or something. I've heard loads of people say, 'When you want to know something, go and see Franco. He's the librarian.'"

By alluding to a reputation, which it never crossed his mind that he possessed, the woman had innocently thrown down a gauntlet. His response to the challenge was to set his brain scampering around to find a way of meeting her curious call for help. After a few minutes, he went to a cupboard, rummaged around, pulled out a recently purchased reference book, glanced over its contents and handed it to her.

"Try looking through this, Signora Ambrosetti," he said. "I reckon that it will give you a few clues about where to turn to next."

Having reaped the benefit of her initial flattering remarks about Franco's much talked about omniscience, Signora Ambrosetti gave him a beatific smile. Though educated by life rather than books, she had the same faith in the man of books as she had in the man of *the* book. She also knew that both were susceptible to female blandishments. As she took the directory, she turned her head to follow Franco's eyes and saw just inside the library entrance three animated, adolescent girls who were chatting, laughing and flailing the air with their long hair. They too wanted to consult Franco but not in his role as librarian.

"Would you please excuse me, Signora? I'll be back in a moment. I need to deal with these young ladies."

Signora Ambrosetti became the audience for what could have been an improvised play: Franco came onto the stage, manoeuvred his way through a rampart of unsorted newspapers and untidily stacked popular magazines that served as a defensive barricade around his desk-cum-castle keep, and made his way across to the girls. On seeing him come towards them, all three, as if in a choreographed movement, jumped in the air, arched their backs and then bent forward to slap their legs. Amidst their exuberant laughter, two of them competed for his attention.

"Franchino! Can you come now? We haven't got long, and we're looking to you for inspiration and guidance!" the shortest of the three pleaded.

"Oh, come off it, Claudia, it's not that urgent. There are still weeks to go," Franco said.

"Well, yes, but you know what I mean. Our exams are coming up, so in fact we don't have that much time," she countered. "We just want you to tell us if we're on the right track. Our *contrada* has got to win the competition this year. San Vincenzo won last time, and we genuinely believe that this year it's our turn. According to Giulia, you said that we ought to paint fragments of a wall onto the canvas."

"Oh, come on. Please, Franco, come and look at what we've done. The colours seem to be all wrong," chirped the girl wearing retro butterfly-winged glasses.

Signora Ambrosetti watched as Franco merged with them and the four bodies flowed out of the main door onto the narrow street and out of sight.

They turned sharp right and down through a narrow passage, which fed into a wider path that formed part of the town's former fortification, passed through an arch and then disappeared into a vaulted cellar. A large piece of light-brown canvas had been stretched taut and pinned to a rectangular wooden frame onto which the girls had painted irregular sections of a brick wall representing a ruined building.

The tallest of the three girls, Silvia, who had so far remained silent, picked up a brush, dipped it into a pot of redbrick-coloured paint and, handed it to him, pouting "Franchino, couldn't you just sketch the outline of what you had in mind? What you suggested last time sounded absolutely brilliant. If *you* do it, after you've gone, we won't argue about what you actually said or what you *really* meant. You can guess what I'm talking about."

While her coquettishness came naturally, her confidence in this case was more contingent, deriving from the fact that she'd been to his simply-furnished bedroom studio (cum-bathroom-sine-kitchen) at the top of his father's house to see his paintings, not once but twice. After her second visit, she had given her friends an embellished account of how, when she had asked him about the book lying open on his bed, he had spent what seemed like an hour telling her about his interest in Greek mythology and how these myths had shaped his approach to life.

She told them then, and would recall later as an adult, how he had helped her to look out of his skylight down onto a small walled enclosure of the former Santuario di Santa Maria degli Angeli; and how he drew her attention to the way the leaning Corsican pines and wild cyclamen had staked their natural claim over the remaining arch; and how he had pointed out the way that the skill and creativity of the stonemason had made the cornerstone of the arch serve as an alcove for a Madonna surrounded by angels. Silvia bit her lower lip at the memory.

Franco, smiling at their high spirits and revelling in their uninhibited expressions of gratitude and exaggerated praise, took the brush and, like an archetypal palette-balancing artist, with a few slow, sweeping arm movements, and with scarcely an uttered word and the barest expenditure of energy, applied the paint with bold, assertive strokes. He completed the task with a theatrical flourish and a broad smile.

"How's that? Is that what you wanted?" he asked.

"Terrific! Now we can finish it off… I've got a clear idea of exactly what we need to do. There'll be no more arguments," Silvia said, jumping and gesticulating. "You're absolutely wonderful, Franco. When we win, we'll let everyone know that our success is down to you."

"You haven't won yet," Franco said as he walked out, adding, "And, if you do, then I'd rather you didn't involve me."

After a few yards, he stopped as if he had suddenly remembered something he had forgotten. As he turned, he saw Silvia looking out of the arch at him. He met her enquiring eye, into which he beamed a creased smile; his thoughts hovered like a darting dragonfly then he slowly pivoted on his heel and sauntered back towards the library.

"I saw you, Franco," said a woman's voice. "She's too young for you." It was Signora Veronese: almost the same height as Franco (and an inch taller than Signor Galgano). The feet of her buttermilk-treated legs were sheathed inside white flat-heeled shoes. She wore no make-up, earrings, bracelets or broaches; her sole adornment was a beaded necklace bought from one of the Senegalese pedlars who ply the sandy beaches of the Maremma.

"I was only doing my bit to improve the chances of their *contrada* winning this year," Franco said, in a tone that was neither defiant nor defensive.

"You all take this spectacle of yours too seriously," she taunted playfully before continuing. "Don't you realise that your attempt to imitate the Siena Palio infantilises you, stops you growing up," she said with a trace of metropolitan conceit. "This annual event is part of the fantasy world you people down here create for yourselves."

"Costanza, we all live on and feed off fantasies. What were the Greek and Roman deities, nymphs and the rest of them if not fantasies, the stuff of our dreams?"

"Not just pleasant dreams, though. Don't forget they're also our nightmares," Costanza interrupted.

"Let's put nightmares away and think instead about pleasant dreams and happy, uplifting fantasies, like those of the young girls back there. You know, what I find puzzling is that it's the teenagers and young adults who are the fantasists. They're the ones who find it romantic to dress up as though they'd just walked out of the *quattrocento*."

"Not just them. Who's been *Il Capitano* of the pageant year after year? Middle-aged Piero," interjected Costanza.

"True, but he's like you, an outsider. He adores the role, especially the dressing up."

"And he likes to wear his own armour, which, excuse the pun, fits his *amour propre,* don't you think?" Costanza asked teasingly.

"Uncalled-for, Costanza."

"I agree. I'm sorry. I do like him. He's a kind-hearted soul and no vainer than most of you Italian males."

"No comment on that last bit. Don't forget that Piero goes to a good deal of effort and expense to make sure that all his armour and other paraphernalia is historically accurate, not just a mishmash from different centuries. He paid quite a bit of money to a top silversmith to make his cuirass, hauberk and helmet. All bespoke stuff. Nothing off the peg for Piero."

"It certainly looks authentic and does fit a treat," said Costanza. "And was it you or someone else who once told me that he also makes a small financial contribution to the whole spectacle?"

"It wasn't me but it's true. He does and for a fairly obvious reason."

"And what's that?"

"He regards what you just called a contribution to be a sort of fee that allows him to keep in with the hunting bunch down here and to join them in the autumn boar shoot. But, listen, Costanza, I can't go on talking now because I've left someone in the library waiting longer than I should have." The soft embrace they gave each other was a reminder of the closeness that had been forged around the time she bought her farmhouse.

"Fine. Shall we have a coffee in the bar tomorrow morning before the library opens?" Costanza asked, lowering her head and smiling.

"Yes. About nine? *Ciao*."

★

He was barely inside the library when the telephone on his desk rang. He walked without rushing towards the sound and, pushing aside a small heap of papers with his arm, snapped up the receiver, imitating the way he saw busy executives act, not in real life but in the cinema. The person at the other end was already talking before Franco had the receiver to his ear. During a pause in the other person's verbal flow, Franco squeezed in the placatory words, "Don't worry. I'll definitely have it ready by Friday evening. It only needs one more coat of oil." At no point during his exchange with his client did he signal to Signora Ambrosetti that he was sorry for the interruption; neither did he make any gesture to convey his impatience or irritation at being disturbed by the caller.

Despite the fact that his librarianship was full-time, salaried and tenured, he found room for his favourite hobby, which was to practise his trade as a highly trustworthy cabinetmaker. And, since he had an established and untarnished reputation, his skills were always in demand. As a result, whenever he accepted a joinery commission, his hobby suddenly became a supplementary income generator. Unfortunately for library users, the boundary between hobby and job became so blurred that periodically his post as librarian transmogrified into being his hobby. When this happened and he was called away, he would put up a notice on the library entrance stating boldly *Back Soon*. This would sometimes prompt one of a particular group of grumpy citizens, who in fact never drew upon the library's facilities, to join with a couple of regular users to grumble and gripe at the librarian's unprofessional behaviour. However, because the Christian admonitions about 'being without sin' and 'casting the first stone' were so deeply embedded in their psyche, no one had ever lodged a formal complaint against him.

From the perspective of Franco, at some point in the future, shortfalls in the municipal budget might compel the local authority to downgrade the librarian's job to part-time status or, worse still, to adopt a policy of using volunteers to staff the library. Therefore, the prescient, logically-thinking philosopher considered it prudent to keep his carpentry work ticking over.

A corollary of his precautionary approach was that his clients felt free to call him at the library at any time, which is precisely what happened when he returned to deal with Signora Ambrosetti. The person at the end of the line was the father of a bride-to-be who wanted Franco's assurance that by the end of the week he would deliver the finished *letto matrimoniale,* which he had commissioned as a nuptial gift as soon as the wedding day had been announced. It never occurred to Franco nor to the client nor, for that matter, to Signora Ambrosetti, that conducting his private business affairs during the library's formal opening hours amounted to an abuse of his position and a non-condonable malpractice.

When he at last put the receiver down, Franco's dismissal of this second interruption with a sweep of the hand evoked not a solitary twinkle of a response from the old lady. Even though he knew that his behaviour was the norm, he felt a gentle tug of guilt at having neglected her for such a long time. In order to assuage his own feelings and, at the same time, offer some compensation to her for his absence, he provided her with a well-seasoned, colourful account of what the girls were up to and what they wanted from him. As a further bonus, he added a few titillating invented, facts about his private client. This he knew was more than enough to satisfy her curiosity and to neutralise any trace of criticism that she might feel towards him.

She bobbed her head as he spoke, accepting his words at face value while simultaneously reading other meanings into them. When he had finished, she gave him another beatific smile, like that of the Madonna universally depicted in paintings and sculptures, and rose to leave with her smile firmly in place. But she was hardly on her feet when the telephone rang, once more interrupting her departure. Fancying that it would be impolite to suddenly disappear, gently rustling her dress, she sat down again and waited to be entertained further.

"Franco, this is Alessandro. I wondered if we could have a coffee together."

"Sure, Alessandro, but not today. Tomorrow will be fine. Could you give me some idea what it's about?"

"Well, there are two things. First, it's about building an extension to the library."

"And the other, more important thing?" Franco knew that something else had to be the real reason for the call.

"It's about my campsite. You've probably heard. The *comune* is planning to close it down because they say I'm contravening health and safety regulations. You and I may not always be in total accord on a whole range of issues, but I'm sure you'd agree that this is a set-up."

"You're right. We do disagree about some things. Not angrily, just fundamentally. But that doesn't stop us being friends. Now, you've asked if I've heard something or other about your campsite. Well, yes, I have, and from what I can gather, the council probably could enforce its closure if they wanted to." Franco paused before adding, "How about meeting around eleven tomorrow?"

"Oh, *dio*!" Alessandro exclaimed down the line. "Franchino, couldn't you make it today? How about my dropping into the library when you close?"

Franco gave in. "*Bene. A più tardi. Ciao.*" He wasn't going anywhere and had vaguely thought of staying on to deal with a few things after closing time. Signora Ambrosetti, who was once more engrossed in the directory Franco had given to her, looked up as he replaced the receiver. It made no difference to her, nor to Franco, that she had listened into this politically-sensitive conversation, for very little took place in the town that didn't sooner or later become public property and a tradable commodity. Artful gossipmongers transformed simple facts of life into minor epics that then drip-fed energy into the inhabitants' daily struggle against the fatigue brought about by doing nothing.

"Francesco, I can't thank you enough. You're amazing. I went through the index in that directory or whatever you call it; the one which you showed me, and I have written down the names of a couple of people that I believe might be able to help us. I can't tell you what my daughter's been going through. This could be the miracle that I've been praying for." Simonetta Ambrosetti stood up and Franco accompanied her to the door. Then turning towards him and putting her hand on his arm, she asked pleadingly: "Can't you come down to give our *contrada* a hand tonight? We need help much more than *La Roca* or *San Vicenzo*. I'll be there with Kristina. I don't think you've seen her since she returned. She's changed an awful lot. You wouldn't recognise her. The ways she looks and dresses. All quite different. Going away as she did has done her the world of good." Because they had both been born in the town and often bumped into one another, Franco understood most of what there was to know about Kristina and could guess what her mother believed to be her daughter's problem.

With his thick black curly hair; clean-shaven face,

exposing well-defined cheekbones; and dark brown eyes, only the mean-spirited would deny that the librarian could be regarded as rather handsome. In the eyes of many women, his stocky – though not muscly – frame gave the impression of both physical vigour and emotional strength. These masculine physical attributes camouflaged his tongue-in-cheek, self-deprecatory wit and sense of irony – an aspect of the man that was most visible and audible whenever he kick-started and drove off on his noisy, vintage 750cc Moto Guzzi.

For a highly imaginative, romantically inclined and well-read older woman, the bike, its rider and the roaring sound of its reverberating and pulsating engine was an invitation to momentarily cast herself as Eurydice in Cocteau's film version of the Orpheus legend. In the mind's eye of such a person, Franco was transformed into the outrider transporting her into the Underworld, a forbidden place that could be virtually anywhere as long as it was outside the town walls, a place where she could indulge her fantasies. Although Signora Ambrosetti did not at all correspond to this description, at the moment she evoked her daughter's name and gazed into Franco's eye, she became that pillion passenger.

"Goodbye, Signora Ambrosetti. I'm glad I was able to help. And, yes, I'll try to drop by later. It all depends. Anyway, as regards miracles, do you know that's the fifth one that's been attributed to me since becoming the librarian?" Franco asked with a suppressed laugh. Then, with a wink to Silvia, who waved to him as she passed the window, Franco escorted the older lady to the door and said with a wide grin, "Don't forget to tell Dom Filippo about the miracle. I don't know why but I think it's time for me to get back into the Church's good books." The rest of the day slipped past quietly and quickly with no further interruptions until seven-thirty, the library's official closing time.

★

Garibaldi's ornately carved, feather-plumed, wide-brimmed hat had barely fallen under the sun's evening shadow than Signor Galgano jogged into the library. He was dressed in a navy-blue sleeveless shirt, creased white shorts and spotlessly clean tennis shoes. Each item of apparel displayed its distinctive designer logo; in the case of the shorts, that of a wild boar. A crown of silvering hair, swept back from a widow's peak, sat above a flushed face and fleshy jowl. Franco was crouched over his desk sorting out newspaper cuttings and placing them in folders. Signor Galgano spoke hoarsely and loudly. Although he rarely shouted, his voice, gravelly through frequent use, always sounded as though he was protesting angrily at something or somebody.

"Franco! Have you seen the notice?"

"No. As I told you earlier, I don't know any more than you do. Someone mentioned in passing that they'd heard that the council had received a complaint about your campsite. Something to do with EU regulations?" In contrast to the older man, Franco spoke so softly that his words were scarcely audible, thus forcing Alessandro to cock his head towards the voice while simultaneously allowing his mouth to droop open as if that would enable him to catch, like a swallow insects in flight, Franco's utterances.

"What sort of complaint and complaint about what? And, just as a matter of interest, who *actually* mentioned it… in passing, as you say?" Alessandro asked while standing akimbo and pushing his face closer to Franco's. "It would be nice to know who the source of this misinformation is. No, sorry. Disinformation, because that's what it is. This person, who is one of those responsible for spreading false and nasty rumours, must be someone who has it in for me."

"Look, Alessandro, are you certain that a formal notice has been pinned to your campsite's gate? I mean, have you been down there yourself? I haven't. I don't need to. It's nothing to do with me," Franco said in a manner that indicated his growing impatience with his interlocutor.

Alessandro ignored the question and carried on: "I never believed they'd do it. It's utterly absurd!"

Franco reached over Alessandro's shoulder and, patting him on his back, said in a manner that was both sympathetic and condescending, "Alessandro, you're letting your paranoia about the *comune* get the better of you."

Alessandro paused and looked down. His natural response to the way Franco had spoken to him was to retaliate. Instead, he mumbled a contrite "No."

"No, what?"

"No. I mean yes, I have been down there, and no. They haven't pinned up a notice." Annoyed with himself for having had to disclose to Franco that there was no evidence for his fear, he came out of his corner of the ring with a jabbing finger. "But you can't call me paranoid! I have received a letter from the *comune*, which I think I'm justified in construing as threatening." Having fought back, he dropped his guard and pulled himself upright from his stooped position.

"So, there you are," said Franco. You have not been excommunicated and your campsite hasn't actually been anathematised, at least not yet," Franco said teasingly.

"Please, Franchino. There are times when your jests aren't funny, only irritating. So, if you don't mind, I wish you'd treat this with the seriousness it deserves."

"For you," Franco murmured.

Alessandro took Franco's interjection in his stride and resumed: "Have you any idea what the complaint is that those bloody officials are looking into? You hinted at it yourself. They're saying that I'm failing to observe the new EU regulations on hygiene in public campsites," Alessandro said, parodying his presumed persecutors while adopting a hand on hip pose. "Do you know what they mean by my 'failing to observe'? I'll tell you. But please listen very carefully because you have to understand the details."

"I can see this is going to take some time, so let's sit down," Franco said with a sigh.

"A good idea," Alessandro said, pulling up a chair.

"Where shall I start? All right, here we go. I've got written approved permission for eighty tents on my site. According to the regulations, I'm expected to have four separate buildings with properly maintained showers, washing and toilet facilities. Can you imagine? My campsite is better provided for than most of our 3-star rated hotels! Each building should have a minimum of five showers and basins."

"And how many do you have?" asked Franco.

"Let me tell you: each building has four, not five, showers and washbasins." Alessandro tilted his head and closed an eye. "Look. You know my camp. Each tent has its own individual niche on a terrace and is separated from the next tent by one, two or, sometimes, even three olive trees. And it has a twenty-five-metre swimming pool. Now, you compare that with Ferraro's dump down there!" He pointed to the bottom of the hill where a rival campsite snuggled into a triangle formed at the point where the road from Montelorenzo intersected with the highway running from Siena to the coast.

"That sod managed to persuade the authorities to let him have ninety-five tents on his site. That means, and everyone knows this, he's only got facilities for one in seven people. Then, on top of all that, his camp is on the flat, so whenever there's a summer downpour, the poor campers are all but washed away. I've had visitors who have stayed down there. Do you know what they call it? Noah's Ark! And, oh, yes, I nearly forgot. His damn swimming pool is only fifteen metres long! Can you imagine?" Signor Galgano's body responded to his

Ciceronian rhetorical flourishes by perspiring.

"They've picked on me as a warning to *him* to behave. What I don't understand is why the people on the council have not raised their concerns directly with him. One person I spoke to yesterday thought that it might be because they're afraid that he might persuade one or two of his regulars to jump to his defence and kick up a fuss in the media. You will know better than me, but I imagine that complaints linking tourism and Montelorenzo coming from any quarter wouldn't go down well with the mayor's office. They wouldn't, would they? Perish the thought!

"There's one couple, who stay there year after year, who would be prepared to take up the cudgel and cause a commotion. I'm sure you know the couple I'm talking about. They're the middle-aged childless duo from Piacenza. They spend ages lounging outside their tent immersed in the contents of a thick book on canine psychology – or so I'm told. Apparently, they're obsessed with wanting to understand the needs of their ancient English cocker spaniel. When the poor thing pops it, they'll both have a mental breakdown and probably divorce." Alessandro gave a belly laugh and, clutching Franco's arm, added: "The next thing we'll hear is that they're both having expensive psychoanalysis supplemented by counselling with a therapist who's a specialist in animal bereavement." Alessandro Galgano was now doubled up, with his hands on his knees and dripping tears. "Recognise them?"

"Yes," Franco chuckled. "But they're harmless and, as far as you're concerned, I don't think that they're the ones you would need to worry about."

"Everyone's talking about them," Alessandro said, his laughter reducing to a nervous snicker.

"I don't know about everyone, but you are," Franco muttered, by now having lost any interest he might have had in Alessandro and the kerfuffle he was making about his campsite.

Having realised that he'd wandered off his main point and that by prattling on he was on course to a demeaning self-destruction, Alessandro stopped talking as suddenly as an April shower, and refocused. His main aim was to corner Franco into agreeing with him on the name of the person who was the main driving force behind what he, Alessandro, considered to be an undeniably real threat to his campsite. But, before he could manoeuvre himself back into the position where he wanted to be, Franco spat the shell of a sunflower seed into his palm and interjected from the corner of his mouth, "Right, Alessandro, it hasn't happened yet, and frankly, if they wanted to be disagreeable and make life difficult for you, they could have put up a large placard announcing their intention to close the site from such and such date. They haven't done so. Let's put it like this: things aren't nearly as bad as they could be. You don't need me to tell you what *you* have to do. You know the person you offended last year. Go and see him and say that you're sorry. You know who I'm talking about, don't you?"

"Yes. That dimwit Stefano Lombardi! And I said what I said because what he did was amazingly stupid, and someone had to tell him. As far as I'm concerned,

I've got nothing to apologise for, so why should I? What does it say about me if I do what you're suggesting? The fact of the matter is that his action was totally brainless. Why? Because the man's an idiot."

Alessandro Galgano had climbed up onto that shaky wooden fence labelled *indignation*. He balanced there for a moment longer to allow his billowing sense of outrage to recede. Then, rather than experience a Humpty Dumpty great fall, he slid down onto the chair of compromise. "All right, have it your way. But please tell me one thing. How should I approach him?" a chastened and dejected Alessandro Galgano asked the librarian.

They walked outside. Franco's advice had a calming effect on the person who was, after all, tantamount to being the library's founder and thus, ironically, Franco's benefactor. Alessandro's arm-waving gradually became more subdued as he resigned himself to the fact that there was no alternative to his going to see the official and eating humble pie. Moreover, he would be doing so in the full knowledge that the offence he had committed lay not in anything that he'd said at the time, but in the fact that his name was Galgano.

★

The Montelorenzene had never fully forgiven Alessandro Galgano's family for what had happened decades ago. Not only had Montelorenzo caught the eye of Garibaldi, but some seventy years later, in 1921, it became home to the first Fascist organisation to be set up in Tuscany, thanks to one local man, Ennio Galgano, Alessandro's uncle. Because of his energetic support for the new political movement, this former Italian Consul in North Africa quickly rose in the hierarchy of the National Fascist Party to become an under-secretary. Although Ennio is a common enough Italian name – Ennius, the Latin name, means 'predestined, God's favourite', and whose Name Day falls on All Saints' Day – he was in fact christened in honour of Quintus Ennius, the first of the great Roman poets and renowned for his prodigious literary versatility. Such was the family's sense of self-importance. After the war, although convicted for having held a high-ranking position in the Fascist Party, he was given a light suspended sentence and proceeded to live in the way to which he had always been accustomed until his death as a very old man in the 1970s.

This legacy gave rise to a resentment that bubbled away in the town's social crust like a suppurating, unhealed lesion. Now and again, however, the flimsiest pretext could be sufficient for this animosity to percolate to the surface and ripple through the community. As far as Alessandro Galgano was concerned, the municipal edict he had expected to find fastened to his campsite gate would be nothing less than the foreshock of a massive earthquake that would destroy what remained of the Galgano patrimony. Although the formal status of this anticipated 'edict' lay in a state of limbo, somewhere between rumour and fact, because Franco had implied that its source might have been a member of a locally influential circle, Alessandro had no doubt that this was a rumour with a solid foundation. In other words, for him to be granted remission (for his sin) it wasn't the Catholic Church that he would have to indulge but the temporal authority.

Alessandro considered that his chat with Franco had been useful for one main reason: it had provided him with a political insider's view of what he should do in order to avert any threat to his campsite being implemented. Nonetheless, invaluable as that information was, he felt that he could benefit from receiving the opinion and advice of an outsider on how to do the minimum necessary to assuage the incubi that were tormenting him. And, therefore, not for the first time when finding himself in conflict with an official who was behaving perversely and whom he could never hope to successfully challenge, he decided to pay Costanza a visit. He could always trust her counsel, especially when his vulnerability derived from his personal and social shortcomings.

★

Alessandro went home and, having neatly placed the few notes and letters he had accumulated during his altercation with the local authority into a folder, left his house fully intending to take the long walk down to Costanza Veronese's farmhouse. However, on closing the door behind him, he changed his mind and instead of turning left, he turned right towards the library. It had suddenly occurred to him that he should have been more effusive in his expression of gratitude to Franco, since, as a member of the Puccini family, the merest support from the librarian was worth having.

On hearing the door open, Franco raised his eyes and emitted a low groan when he saw Alessandro toddling towards him with a grin like that of a waxing crescent moon, revealing a set of bright white teeth and a tucked-away black space waiting to be filled. His visitor's jovial manner both surprised and worried him, since the cause of such an outward transformation in the campsite owner over such a brief span of time was beyond his ken.

"*Ciao*, Alessandro, what brings you back? From the look on your face, it must be good news," was all that Franco could manage to say, closing the newspaper he was reading and standing up.

"Francesco, I've something that I'd like to talk to you about," Alessandro began, in the tone that an older person adopts when they're about to present a homily to someone younger. "It's been on my mind on and off for quite a while and it occurred to me that now was a good moment to get it off my chest. Let me start by reassuring you that it's nothing for you to be anxious about."

"I see," said Franco. "Then spit it out, old chap, if it will make you feel better," Franco said, in a tone that matched the facetiousness of his choice of words.

Alessandro drew up a chair, placed it in front of the desk – behind which Franco continued to stand, conspicuously fiddling with a pencil – and slowly lowered himself down. He put his hands behind his head and stretched out his legs. "Would you like to sit down for a moment, please, Franco," Alessandro suggested, as a superior might to a subordinate, pointing to the chair behind which Franco was still standing.

The librarian gave a prolonged blink of astonishment at this ostensible instruction. Despite being intensely irritated, he did as he was beckoned and then retaliated by leaning forward, placing his elbows on the desk, interlocking his fingers and twiddling his thumbs. Each small, slow, deliberate movement was supposed to convey his growing feeling of resentment towards the way that Alessandro had virtually usurped his office.

However, the visitor's lack of response indicated either that he was oblivious to the message that Franco was eager to communicate, or that he had decided to take no notice of the librarian's non-verbal signal of his annoyance. For one long minute, he sat without moving, his head bowed down looking at his podgy fingers, like a judge pondering his words before passing judgement. Then he raised his head, took a deep breath, smacked his lips, rode back on two legs of his chair and began slowly: "Since I'm quite a bit older than you, Franchino, and because I've known you all your life, I have – what can I say? – a sort of avuncular feeling towards you."

Franco raised his eyebrows, scratched his arm, opened his mouth as if to speak and then closed it. All his facial expressions and body movements this time signalled not so much indignation at his neighbour's behaviour as his incredulity at what he was hearing. In truth, he shouldn't have been quite so surprised, because Alessandro was well-known for his bewildering turns of phrase, his malapropisms and embarrassing obiter dicta. He would float the most outlandish ideas and then commit an astonishing acrobatic volte-face.

"The other day, I was wondering about – how should I put it? – you getting married," Alessandro began. "You know, you're a very eligible bachelor, and I've often noted how well your silent charm works on women of all ages."

Franco uncrossed his legs – at least he now knew where he stood, more or less – rested back in his chair and, looking Alessandro in the eye, said, "You don't want me to propose to your daughter, do you?"

"Good gracious, no! Of course not," Franco's newly acquired Uncle Alessandro cried, his mouth dropping.

"What do you mean by 'Of course not'?" enquired Franco, with a histrionic display of grievous hurt. "Are you saying that she's too good for me? You are, aren't you? That's what you're saying."

Franco had been so terrified at the mention of marriage that his adrenalin gland had immediately begun to release its hormones at a rate reserved for those in fear for their lives. It was this that had caused him to flush and respond so aggressively.

"No, no, Franco, you're misunderstanding me," Alessandro said, reaching over the desk to pat his notional nephew's hand. "Please allow me an *éclaircissement*."

Smarting from a class-righteous sense of injury, the librarian puffed out his cheeks and then slowly exhaled – a behavioural technique which gave him time to recover his composure. He picked up his pencil and poked it at Alessandro Galgano. "Alessandro, do you think that your pursuit of Costanza Veronese is going to get you anywhere? The only thing that the two of you have in common is that she's from the same town as the founder of the party of which your uncle was a leading light. The difference between her family and yours is that hers resisted the pressure to follow the chrome-domed Fascist brute." Alessandro was not even tempted to retaliate, for he could read in Franco's eyes the younger man's feeling of class vulnerability, of being at this moment a Puccini foot soldier thrusting his spear at the Galgano knight's escutcheon.

Alessandro's rather innocent idea, when put into words, had left them both momentarily bruised. Both of them had overreacted, and now it was too late for Alessandro to rescue and pursue his far-fetched and fanciful idea. While he gloomily retraced his word-steps through the silence between them, Franco for his part was beginning to feel that he had been overhasty in his judgement of what Alessandro had intended to say. His wounding words had been a spontaneous response to what he had experienced as a psychological blow to his ego; his cutting reaction also revealed his ambivalence about Alessandro's treatment by the municipal authorities. He didn't bear any personal grudge against the man, and history had already passed judgement on the Galganos. Since the local power now exercised by Franco's family trumped Alessandro's status, Franco, as an ordinary non-vindictive human being, quickly concluded that it was for him to show remorse and make the first move to restore peace between them. He did so by that simple human act that has evolved with *Homo sapiens* to undo such tangled knots of tension – to laugh loudly.

Alessandro pounced on Franco's primordial signal by standing up, going around to Franco's side of the desk and throwing his arms around him. The laugh and the embrace signalled that the storm had passed over. The needle on the barometer of their relationship returned to the steady position that existed before they had stumbled into the emotionally charged gorse thicket of social class origin.

The older man's basic impetuosity had led him to create a half-baked vision of himself as a counsellor-cum-confidant to this younger man. Even if Franco did not reflect any further upon the issue of marriage, he might nonetheless show his appreciation for the thought Alessandro had given to the matter on his behalf – for instance, by speaking out in his favour should the issue of his campsite ever arise when he was in the company of people with fingers on the policy decision-making button. In the end, it was Alessandro who rescued the day for both of them by admitting, "How silly of me. It was just an idea. You getting married? What a joke!"

*

Franco's mother had died at a relatively early age, long before he became the librarian. Fortunately for him, he had an elder sister who, despite having her own full-time job in the post office, looked after him and his brother, Antonio, as well as their father. Her life improved marginally and for a short time when Antonio married and left home. It worsened again when she married and moved downstairs into the flat her brother had vacated, for she now had to cater for two separate households; that of her father and that of her younger brother, Franco. The birth of a child not long afterwards saw her conditions of service deteriorate further. The men, all of whom carried the membership card of the same progressive Left, with its pledge to stop exploiting the labour of others, were blind to their own blatant exploitation of the person who was daughter, sister and wife.

Then, one day, her father, more adventurous than his younger son, Franco, decided that, since his daughter's time and attention had become too dissipated to be able to look after him to the standard to which he was accustomed, he had no choice but to remarry. Being an eligible widower, it wasn't long before he found a person of corresponding status, a widow in a neighbouring town. It was a good match, and the ideal Italian conjugal symbiosis was soon restored. Within months of the installation of a new regime in his father's household, Franco celebrated his thirty-fifth birthday.

The coincidence of the marriage and his birthday presaged change in Franco's life. Hitherto, as the baby of the family, when it came to accommodating to changes in the lives of other members of the household, he had only ever been obliged to make minor adjustments to his routines and to his use of the domestic space. Kind and rather introspective, and neither acquisitive nor aspirational, Franco lived a contented existence. Though not a virgin, he had never been promiscuous and his onanism was commensurate with a low libido. He had had three lengthy sexual relationships, two of which he freely accepted could justly be described as languid and lacking in intensity and for whose outcome he claimed full or at least partial responsibility, depending on to whom he was speaking.

The first was a typical late-teen romance with Donatella, a young woman and, like him, a native of Montelorenzo whom he had met at kindergarten. No sooner had she reached puberty than her mother began drilling into her that she must do everything that she could to avoid following in her footsteps and, instead, set her mind firmly on making a success of life. By the time she sat her *matura,* Donatella had fully surveyed the choices open to her and discerned in Franco the best vehicle for her to blossom and achieve her ambition to become well-to-do and lead an exciting social life. She and Franco began to cuddle in the summer before he went to university, and their romance continued throughout his student years spent on and off in the Eternal City.

It was only after he had graduated and returned home permanently that she experienced the sense of foreboding that he was not, after all, the person destined to help her escape from what would otherwise be her natural birthright, which she figuratively described as life in a stagnant well. She had accumulated more than enough evidence to conclude that life with Franco would, regrettably, not be one of material affluence, excitement and fun. She had never bothered to find out what Franco had meant when he declared himself to be a sort of imperfect Stoic and who was ever ready to quote Marcus Aurelius's famous dictum, 'A person has power over their mind but not outside events'. Donatella had finally realised that his approach to life did not sit comfortably with her own mother-induced homespun philosophy. At the kernel of her world view was the principle that a life full of tragedy would be infinitely more fulfilling than the boring repetitiveness of the quotidian which, most of the time, did nothing other than turn the town's life-long inhabitants into cobblestones.

Franco's other significant relationship was an adulterous affair with an older woman, Adriana, who owned a shop in another town. This liaison had dripped along for almost a year until Franco's conspicuous lassitude pushed them towards a classical tragi-comical denouement. A few days after they had kissed and parted, following another flabby, shabby evening together, he received a short letter from her informing him that she had plumped to remain with her (equally humdrum but nonetheless tolerable) husband in their mesh of extended family and friends.

Franco wrote back a few days later expressing his regret that things had not worked out for them and reproached himself for not showing greater understanding of the risky situation in which their clandestine relationship had placed her. He concluded by saying that he fully understood why she had made her decision, apologised for his inadequacies and wished her happiness. After he had dropped the letter into the postbox, he gave a thankful sigh of relief.

In between these two lacklustre romances, there had been the stunningly beautiful, captivating Simonetta: the only woman with whom he had become stupefyingly infatuated. He surrendered himself to her and she absorbed him. At the time, rather than wishing and hoping, he convinced himself that his feelings were reciprocated and that they were equally besotted with one another. But they were not reciprocated; the relationship had from early on been entirely one-sided. He had been so committed to her that he lost the ability to think and act without flagellating himself in his striving to imagine what she would want. When she brusquely announced that she needed to terminate what he liked to call their 'affective bond', his cultivated stoicism was unable to prevent him from sinking into depression. The manner in which she had so abruptly and heartlessly exited his life left him so bruised and dazed that it took him almost a year to recover.

Apart from these affairs, there had been a bare handful of sexual encounters. A couple had left him with pleasant memories, while the vapidity of another and the painfulness of the Simonetta episode disinclined him to expend any more of his limited energy rummaging around in the marketplace of carnal desire. At the same time, he enjoyed being the librarian and putting his artisan skills to use whenever they were called upon.

As a result of these negative and positive charges, he concluded that he led a rather full life and therefore had no cause to worry about not living conventionally with another person. Instead, like Adriana, he chose to satisfy his emotional needs inside a comforting circle of siblings, other relatives and friends.

★

The decision by Franco's father to remarry worked out splendidly for himself but not so satisfactorily for Franco. In the years before remarrying, Franco's stepmother had grown used to her widowhood and had forgotten that looking after one man full time could be tiring. So, when she accepted old man Puccini's proposal, she had not expected that she would also have to deal with the run-of-the-mill routine, but nonetheless additional, claims made on her by *his* bachelor son. After all, besides caring for father and son Puccini, she still had to attend to the periodic calls upon her time made by her own grown-up children and grandchildren, who lived a bus ride away.

Although Franco never received anything vaguely approaching a reprimand for what he had or had not done, his stepmother was adept at dropping hints of varying degrees of subtlety about what tasks she considered fell outside her remit. After a few weeks as mistress of the household, all of a sudden, his washing, which he had placed in the laundry basket as usual, was left unwashed; his empty tube of toothpaste wasn't replaced; the sheets weren't changed, and his room wasn't cleaned. At first, such signals indicating what she regarded as his responsibility related solely to his personal sphere and effects. Then, incrementally, over a short space of time, she finalised the delineation of her territorial domain.

For instance, the cat, which she had brought with her, liked to curl up in Franco's favourite armchair. Whenever he gently dislodged the creature in his stepmother's presence, she would tut-tut and make an exaggerated show of picking the animal up and sitting it on her lap. She would also fussily pat the cushions immediately after Franco had stood up to leave the room. Though it never occurred to him to enter any of these small environmental changes into a ledger, his nostrils sensed that, since there appeared to be less and less oxygen in the atmosphere for all three people to inhale effortlessly, he was at risk of suffocating in the fading fabric of their communal space.

Fortunately, the diminished capacity to breathe did not stop them huffing and puffing in unison over both minor domestic and broader family matters. Even when the air grew thunderous, eventually being split by an outburst of disagreement over whether the behaviour of another politician should be judged hypocritical or venal, personally hurtful words were never spoken. At larger family gatherings, it was quite common for someone to retell an anecdote about Franco and the family home. And all three of them teased him that the midwife had delivered him in that house and a priest would probably see him leave it. Although such words as 'unwanted' or 'unwelcome' were never used, Franco could not escape feeling that, to put it bluntly, he was simply 'in the way'.

★

Early one morning, Franco mounted his Guzzi and rode down to a nearby village to meet a newly acquired client, who had commissioned him to repair an antique walnut chest of drawers. At mid-morning, he drove back to the library to put up a notice informing would-be users that the library would open after lunch – a vague time somewhere between three-thirty and five. As he was writing the note, he felt a tap on his shoulder. It was Costanza.

"*Ciao*, Franco. Since I had to come up to see your cousin, who I regret to say is behaving badly yet again, I thought I'd drop in on you rather than give you a call. But tell me, won't he ever grow up?"

"Oh, I doubt it."

"Well, he should. He makes such a fool of himself. Anyway, that's by the bye. Now, first of all, let me say I'm ever so sorry to disturb you in your office because I know you're always busy." Costanza paused. "That's supposed to be a joke."

"It's one I'm used to hearing," Franco said, shrugging off the mocking undertone of her statement as unintentional.

"Oh, come on. I'm not being serious. You're doing a brilliant job."

"That too is what I'm accustomed to hearing people say to me, after they've made what they have come to recognise was an unwelcome remark on their part. So, let's change the subject. What is it you want to talk about?"

"It's poor old Alessandro. He's got himself into a real state about this campsite business. And, apparently, from what I've heard, he has good reason to be worried. I mean, is it true that he could be in quite serious trouble with the *comune*? Whether it's true or not, it's getting the poor fellow down badly."

"What do you need to see Fausto for?" Franco asked, instead of addressing Costanza's question.

"Don't be nosy. But, if you must know, I'm not that happy with his latest designs for my outbuildings. Is that enough to keep you going?" she said quite sharply, and then smiled.

"Planning permission could be difficult," Franco said knowingly.

"That, as you might have guessed, is precisely why I asked him to take it on as a project in the first place. He is a Puccini too, among many other things," Costanza replied testily.

"So, Alessandro," Franco said, almost impatiently, "I'm afraid I haven't got time to stop and have a long chat about it now. All I can say is that I recommended a course of action he could take. Though, to be quite frank, he knows full well to whom he's got to go and apologise."

"Yes. He told me. I think you gave him a sound piece of advice."

"And? But look, rather than stand out here, let's go inside for a minute." Franco put up the note and relocked the door behind them.

Costanza began: "The poor man followed your suggestion, made an appointment to see this particular official, went to see him and was spot on time. But this pettifogging clerk kept him waiting for over forty minutes and when he at last called Alessandro into his office, the blighter behaved abominably. Not even so much as a 'I'm sorry I kept you waiting.' I'm sure that we can both picture the situation. You know, when for some reason you have no option other than to go and see a public official, what do you find?"

"If you're unlucky, the chances are you'll find yourself looking into the face of a petty tyrant who takes great delight in lording it over others whenever the opportunity arises."

"Quite. Absolutely right. Of course, there are exceptions, but this wasn't one of them. In this case, the fellow probably relished watching Alessandro grovel. I don't know whether grovel is the right word, but that's the word that Alessandro used. To be honest, we all know how he can exaggerate. But putting aside that particular foible and his paranoia, the outcome of the meeting was exactly as he expected. He knew before he made the appointment, the sole purpose of which was to apologise, that a verbal repentance would never be enough. Lombardi, I think that's his name, made it unsubtly clear that he wants Alessandro to express his regret in other more tangible ways. You know what that implies."

"I suppose so," Franco said, sitting down and resting his head in the cup of his hand.

"Not suppose. You know so. Alessandro's better acquainted with the rules than most people. In this case, though, he's playing in the dark. He's sure that the owner of the other campsite has greased someone's palm and has probably promised other favours too."

"Fine. Well, not fine, but still a realistic assessment. What do you want me to do about it?"

"It seems to me that, basically, you and Alessandro get on very well."

"Don't exaggerate," Franco said.

"All right, not very well, but more than just quite well. Is that better?"

Franco nodded and Costanza continued.

"Look, over the years, you've done one another favours and you never know when he might be able to do something special for you beyond a small favour. You live in the same small town but belong to and move in different social circles. You can exercise some influence in Lombardi's circle, and maybe one day Alessandro will be able to pick up the phone and speak on your behalf to someone in one of his circles."

"I don't see how," Franco countered.

"Neither do I," Costanza responded. "That's one of the beauties of life, don't you think? Its unpredictability. We don't really know what's going to happen next."

"That's certainly true of our economy. It operates like one great casino. At the same time, our politics from top to bottom is another type of casino – a total mess," Franco butted in.

"I was thinking about the likes of us, the ordinary

man or woman in the street, not about those responsible for the big mess-ups in society. All we can ever say to one another is 'You never know.' It's one of my favourite expressions and I leave you with it: you never know. Ah, just one more thought. It's about time that old lefties like you and right-wingers like Alessandro threw away your old-fashioned portmanteaux full of worn-out and surprisingly similar ideas."

"Oh, yes?" Franco sighed. "As I'm the librarian, almost the secular keeper of souls, the guardian of the tree of knowledge, I'm always open to being enlightened."

"Well, to start with, both of you are locked into ways of thinking about the world that led you to shout in the streets and screech over the rooftops about the 'New Man' and the 'New Order'. These ideas are dead, and both of you would benefit by dumping the stillbirth remains."

"That's nice to know," Franco said, turning up the corners of his mouth in a sardonic smile. "But what is it exactly that you're suggesting we used to believe in?"

"Well, for you and for me, for example, it's the idea that we could achieve a society where there was less inequality and more social justice. Have you forgotten those people in our camp who even talked of a classless society? What a ridiculous idea that turned out to be! If we're honest about it, those ideas have all but been totally abandoned, don't you think? As for Alessandro, well, he's up his bum with the comical notion that we're about to witness the revival of the ancient Roman Empire," Costanza said wryly.

"To bring you up to date on Alessandro's position, I can tell you that he's downsized his ambition for the empire. Now Italy only stretches from Rome to the Danube."

They both laughed. "I'll leave you to put up your note. What's it going to say? Back later? Or back tomorrow?"

"Later."

They left together. She went into the shop opposite the library and he stuck his note on the door and walked across the piazza to where his Guzzi was parked.

*

Franco had almost finished giving a final polish to a chest of drawers in his workshop, a rented garage in the middle of nowhere, when the alarm on his wristwatch announced that it was twelve-thirty and thus time to stop for lunch. Had he started the job at the time he had intended, the chest would be ready for collection and he would be on his way back to Montelorenzo. Instead, he went into the yard, climbed onto his Guzzi and drove a short distance to a snack bar next to the level crossing on the mainline railway track between Rome and Livorno.

His passing comment to a young woman standing at the counter, made with his mouth half full after taking a large bite from his *panino*, had not been particularly witty, yet she had responded with a cheerful giggle. In doing so, she exposed between her full but not thick lips a set of slightly irregular teeth with a tantalising gap between the central incisors. She had ringleted chestnut brown hair and strikingly calm sea-green eyes. Her slender frame was covered by a loose-fitting, low-cut, front-buttoning floral cotton dress.

The barman brought up the story dominating the local and regional news, which was Montedison's announcement that it was planning to demolish the barber-pole chimney as part of the company's strategic review of its global operations. The public response was predictable: on the one hand stood those who welcomed the removal of the eyesore, while on the other were those who condemned any such decision which, they pointed out, would mean significant cutbacks in the firm's local activities, with the inevitable corollary of severe job losses. All three of them agreed that the future looked grim not only for those made redundant, regardless of their skills or gender, but also for school-leavers and other youngsters who had enrolled on courses in the different nearby colleges, anticipating that they would find work at the plant.

Franco chipped in with a remark about the influx into the area of rich Italians from the north and Germans (from still further north) who, attracted by the countryside and the climate, might generate jobs in the local economy. The barman added that on existing evidence, it would be poor immigrants from the south who would take these low-wage jobs, mainly in agriculture and the service sector, by bidding down the wage at which they would be willing to work.

"What do you mean by 'south'?" asked the woman. "Do you mean the south of Italy?"

"Yes," said the barman wiping the top of the bar.

"It depends on the sector," Franco added. "In some sectors, the south means south of the Sahara."

Their jostling voices gradually came to the boil, and the brew that poured out of the teapot spout was a rambling informal discourse about immigrants in general. In the end, they all shook their heads, indicating a sense of despair, and generally concurred that immigrants should not take the blame for the sad state that the country found itself in.

One of the regulars standing beside them was a man with a shaven head, pencil-thin moustache and matching manicured tuft of hair in the cleft of his chin. He took out a cigarette, slipped off his bar stool and, wiping crumbs off his shirt, admonished them like some ancient soothsayer to beware of the future. When he went outside for a smoke, the young woman made a couple of comments about her job and migrants and the positive and negative aspects of the financial sector in which she worked. Franco expressed his vexation with the feuding left-wing factions and his DNA-deep suspicion about the new coalition of the Right. The barman preferred not to reveal his personal electoral preference and went off to serve a couple of other customers.

Franco and the young woman exchanged names. She was called Nadja. Time passed. The unseasonal nature of the weather was touched upon, and they expressed similar criticisms about the rising price of food and cost of accommodation. Nadja looked at her watch, drained her cup, let her dangling leg touch the floor and with a friendly smile and a *buon giornata* to Franco and the barman went outside onto the road just as the bus arrived. Throughout the short ride back to her office, Nadja replayed in her head the opening bars of a catchy tune that had been popular throughout the previous summer.

After work, she went for a walk with one of her few close friends, who worked for a small start-up company which leased rooms above Nadja's bank. She described to her in detail her lunchtime encounter with a mild-mannered, quietly spoken, quirky Moto Guzzi biker and the feelings that it had generated in her.

"Did you arrange to meet again?" the friend asked.

"No, but who knows, we might run into one another somewhere or other," Nadja said as they linked arms.

*

When it came to giving birth to her first child, Nadja's mother – who had moved north to Tuscany with her husband, a mining engineer – returned to the overcrowded family home in one of the Mezzogiorno's depopulated towns where her sister and other female relatives lived. Following a late Caesarean section, delays in diagnosing the symptoms she was exhibiting as septicaemia and then further mistakes in initiating the treatment led to organ failure and death. Nadja, who survived childbirth, later discovered that, though the death rate from sepsis was extremely low, in Italy it was the second cause of direct maternal mortality.

Her father was granted permission by his employer to take unpaid leave to attend his wife's funeral and was present at the baptism of his daughter, whom he had named Nadezhda, or Nadja for short. She was her father's hope for the country's future; a girl who would grow up to be an emancipated woman in a world that had broken with the past; a girl who, with her narrow hips, could have been a boy. Her androgynous physique was itself a metaphorical cloak for many of her feelings, some of which lay on the open access shelf of her mind to be picked up and pored over whenever her thoughts floated away from the page, screen or scene in front of her. Like most people, she also harboured deeply buried and unreachable emotions. Between these extremes was one that, though accessible, she preferred not to explore. This was her anxiety that the fragile body she inhabited was the outward manifestation of an inner conflict between the values of the Church, which she rejected but willy-nilly imbibed, and those of her communist father.

For many years, she remained in the South, where she was brought up principally by her mother's sister with whom she lived, hundreds of miles away from her father. Fortunately for their relationship, he never remarried and did what he could to ensure that they remained in close contact. Every year, he travelled south to spend Christmas with them and each summer holiday she and her aunt stayed with him in a village not far from Montelorenzo.

When she reached secondary school age, both she and her aunt moved to join him permanently.

Nadja was, from the kindergarten phase of her existence, a quiet, rather booky child, someone who preferred to stay at home rather than play with other children. After reading Camus in her mid-teens, she would at times, as adolescents do when in an introspective mood, mutter to herself, 'je suis l'étranger.' While in some senses she was by definition an outsider, she was never ever really a loner, and certainly not a recluse. Encouraged by her father, she attended a specialist secondary school, the Liceo Scientifico, a long bus ride away from her home.

While a student there, she spent a good deal of her limited leisure time with three of the only five females in her year, all of whom at that point in their lives wanted to go on to study sciences at university. Quite unconsciously, she lived the virtue of the 'I-Thou' relationship propounded by Martin Buber which, when translated into actual behaviour, meant that she usually met each of her friends alone, one at a time. Her preferred self-description was that she was a person who was at heart unsociable but at the same time socially skilled. By this, she meant that, although she had no great desire to socialise, she had an aptitude for making friends. This facility enabled her to convince people that she really liked the company of others, especially of those with whom she was at that moment engaging.

By the end of the first term of the Laurea Triennale in the nearby university's engineering department, she switched to operational management, which was taught as an adjunct course to engineering. On graduation, she applied to Montedison to work in its personnel section.

★

For eight years she had been married to Fabrizio, a man who shared her father's Communist aspirations. He too believed that their relationship should be of two equal individuals, who had embarked on a shared odyssey as independent human beings. Looking back, he came to see that, from the very beginning of their relationship, they had not been an owl and a pussy cat happily setting sail in a pea-green boat. It was not long into their marriage that it became clear to both of them that they held diametrically opposed views on that most fundamental choice that virtually every couple, who are spoken of by their friends as an 'item', has to confront – that of becoming parents. Nadja was adamant that she did not want to become pregnant, and the option of adopting a child was never discussed; in fact, it had never even crossed their minds.

In late-night bathroom-mirror confessionals, Fabrizio reluctantly admitted to subscribing to the belief that it was in a woman's nature to want to become a mother – the corollary of which was that by behaving as nature required, the woman would allow the male to fulfil *himself* and become a father. For a significant minority of the population in late twentieth-century Italy, this amounted to heresy.

The alter ego that listened so attentively to his confession only aggravated the increasing resentment he felt towards his wife. This, in turn, incubated in her a terrifying neurosis. Her stifled anguish manifested itself in her wasting body and in unpredictable emotional outbursts. Eventually, as she retreated in panic from her husband and into herself, confused by her failure to understand why she felt as she did, he moved from pleading lachrymosely to impatiently demanding (with the cowled figure of his mother behind him) that she fulfil her marriage vow to give him the children that he (and his family) wanted.

As their youthful and fertile Garden of Eden turned into the Negev Desert, they agreed to separate. After the distressful but purifying pyre had consumed both their petty discontents and heftier, more intense despondencies, they parted with barely a soupçon of acrimony. When she finally, decisively left – and there is only one such moment – she put inside her handbag, besides the usual lipstick and compact mirror, all her unarticulated and unresolved feelings; above all, the memory of her mother's death.

As a gesture to herself, husband, friends and neighbours that the breakdown of their relationship was irrevocable, she moved from the village in which she had spent most of her life to a rented three-roomed flat in a nearby seaside resort, which she shared with her mother's unmarried sister, who was also her godmother and to whom she had always been close. Having initially moved in with the aim of supporting her niece during her first summer alone, Nadja's aunt had then stayed on so that she could be nearer the hospital where she was receiving treatment. At the time of her encounter with Franco, Nadja had been divorced from her husband for nearly two years.

★

Less than a month after their chance encounter, by mutually longed-for coincidence, Nadezhda and Francesco bumped into one another again, in the same bar at almost the same time of day. As she came in, Franco put down the bar's copy of the local newspaper that he was reading, not for information but as a way of killing time. He pushed away the small two-chair table at which he was sitting, stood up and used the standard opening gambit.

"*Ciao*," he said.

"*Ciao*," she replied.

"Good day at the office?" he asked.

"Much as normal," she replied.

"I'm just about to order. Fancy joining me?"

"Yes. Sure. Why not? Though I don't have too much time," Nadja said, cocking her head.

"What would you like?"

They chatted, jested and ate. At one point, Nadja looked at her wrist, saw no watch and after asking Franco for the time, added: "I must keep my eye on the clock. Can you tell me when it's two-thirty? The bus comes at two thirty-five and I don't want to miss it."

They continued talking. Franco forgot to look at his watch, and since she forgot to ask him, she missed the bus. Neither of them had heard it arrive and as no one else was waiting at the stop, they only heard it when it sailed past. They rushed out in a token gesture, behaving exactly as a playwright of such a scene would have prescribed in his stage notes for the play's producer.

Franco appeared unperturbed and said in the calmest of voices: "I'll tell you what – I'll ask the barman if I can borrow his helmet. I know he has one. Then I'll give you a lift into town. Your bank is more or less around the corner from my workshop and so I can drop his headgear off on my way home, since it's on one of my routes back to Montelorenzo."

"You're joking. From what you told me, my office is miles from where you have to be. Surely, your client will be expecting to meet you at your workshop at the time you agreed," Nadja protested softly, crinkling her forehead.

"Oh, don't worry. He knows me and my attitude to time. I'm never really late," Franco said breezily.

"Late is late. But what's *really* late?"

"Time's a human invention. I've never knowingly let the clock govern my life and never look back to see if it's catching me up either. But everyone's ultimately satisfied with what I do and no one has ever complained."

"Never?"

"Once."

"Only once?"

"Twice."

"Was it because you failed to deliver on time?"

"No. Nothing to do with time, and in both cases the two individuals involved withdrew their complaints. If you really want to know what happened, I'll explain another time. But I can assure you that you'll find both incidents as boring to listen to as they will be for me to recount."

"Fair enough. Another time, that's if we have the time." Nadja tittered. "I still think that your idea that time is an invention and therefore there's no need to run your life by the clock could be risky and cause you problems. At least sometimes. Haven't you ever stopped to wonder what you might have missed or lost or left behind?" Nadja asked with a smile and a quizzical frown.

"Sounds Proustian. But we'd better not let him join in, because if we do then you'll definitely be late returning to your office," Franco said over his shoulder as he ambled back to the bar. He returned with a helmet and they walked outside to his bike.

"Hop on. You can be my Eurydice."

"Who?" Nadja asked.

"Just trying to be funny. But, seriously, when we're on the bike, don't talk to me because, unlike some motorcyclists, I never turn my head when I'm driving."

Nadja rolled her eyes in disbelief at the situation and at whatever it was that he was saying. She reached behind her to hold the pillion bar. When they reached the main road, Franco gave his bike's powerful engine full throttle. It was on a long straight that they overtook the bus she would have caught. Knowing the town like some mothers do the nits in their child's hair, he drove directly to where she worked. She dismounted, shook out her hair and returned the helmet. Franco asked her whether she'd like to see the Montelorenzo main event of the year that was to take place on the following weekend. She laughed and said yes.

"I'll come and pick you up, if you like," he said.

"Great. At what time? Oops, I forgot – time doesn't mean much to you," she said gleefully.

"About eleven," Franco replied with a smile.

"So, between ten and twelve on Saturday or Sunday?" she said teasingly.

"All right, let's make it Saturday at eleven-thirty."

★

When they arrived in Montelorenzo, a large section of the town's population and quite a few tourists were applauding loudly as the contenders in the pageant strolled out through the main gate of the castle keep and onto a small area of scorched grass. They were led by a young couple, dressed in costumes of the *quattrocento* and the colours of their *contrada,* which had won the competition. Franco guided Nadja by her forearm from the car park to a small hillock above the display of banner tossing that they were about to watch.

On seeing Costanza diagonally across the dusty, forlorn arena from where they stood, Franco shifted his position minimally to take himself out of her line of vision. As his eye roved around the crowd, he saw much nearer to them Silvia in the colours of San Vincenzo, whose *contrada* had taken the prize for the most original theme and for the way it had been presented. She was looking at him and, catching his eye, smiled and waved. At that moment when he returned her smile, Nadja turned to ask him a question, but changed her mind. After a while, Franco, judging that the flag twirling, throwing and catching had lasted long enough and was coming to a close, touched her gently at the waist and guided her through the crowd.

As they walked back to the Guzzi, Nadja couldn't stop herself from remarking, "You seem to be well known to all the most attractive young girls."

"All? Are you thinking of that one schoolgirl who waved? Oh, she's my niece."

"In the village I came from, virtually everyone was a cousin, niece or nephew or great-nephew. So, how close is she?" Nadja felt impelled to persist.

"Not that close. Let me think. Ah, she must be my sister's husband's niece." The preciseness of their relationship tripped off Franco's tongue. He didn't know for certain if his description was correct but had no doubt that they were distantly related.

Before the train of conversation on which they were travelling could gather pace and head towards a place – not a wide, never-ending beach but a cul-de-sac, where neither wanted to end their journey – Franco felt a strong hand grip his arm. It was Piero, the pageant's *Capitano del Popolo*, dressed in a corselet, his neck encased in a white ruff and over his shoulder a short, black, embroidered velvet gown. A helmet was tucked under his arm and a sheathed sword with an ornate handle hung from his belt. The middle-aged Piero, with his trimmed grey hair and beard, looked as though he had been posing for an advertisement. A professional goldsmith, he had an established reputation for crafting plates and chalices engraved with the heraldic crest of people rich enough to commission him.

"*Ciao*, Franco," the master of the guard almost bellowed. "Come and join me for a drink. And who is this lovely lady you're with?"

"Piero, this is Nadja. Nadja lives in Gerfalco. Piero lives in Turin."

After Franco's brief introduction, Piero guided them through a passageway and up a flight of steps to his rented flat on the first floor of a four-storey house. The lounge was modestly but stylishly furnished; a tapestry adorned one wall and a threadbare rug added colour to a sheeny floor of variegated yellowish-brown flagstones. Piero made and poured them coffee. They chit-chatted easily and could have gone on, but Piero had to call time, explaining that he had his captain's duties to perform. At this stage in the day's events, this required him to do no more than meander around, mingle with the crowd and smile benignly.

As Franco stood up, Piero put his hand on his shoulder and said, "There's one small point that I did want to raise with you, Franco, and I'm awfully glad that it didn't slip my mind altogether. It's something that I picked up about Alessandro Galgano and his campsite."

"I can imagine what it might be," Franco said.

"I haven't got time now, but could you tell me all about it, say, tomorrow? We could have lunch together." Piero smiled at Nadja, opened the front door for her and stepped back. When they emerged into the sunlight, he put his arm around her and said with a wink, "This man here is not just good-looking. In fact, I've heard more than one person comment on how, from different angles, he has a strong likeness to Ninetto Davoli. You know who I mean, don't you? Pasolini's favourite actor and, ahem, former lover? But unlike Davoli, Franco is a man of many talents. He's not just a philosopher – anyway, we're all one of those – but he's also not a bad artist. If you want to judge how good or bad, you can go and see two of his paintings that are hanging in the new restaurant that's recently opened in what used to be the convent of San Lorenzo. The place is a bit expensive – but then it would have to be if it's to pay the prices that Franco charges for his artistic endeavours."

"Really. That expensive?" Nadja frowned, though rather thrilled at the thought.

"Well, everything's relative, isn't it? Anyway, seeing his paintings is one thing, hearing him sing is another. Has he sung to you yet?"

"No," said Nadja, raising her eyebrows.

"He's got a fantastic voice. That's his real gift, singing. I've told him often enough that if he ever fell on hard times and wanted to, then he could earn his living as a singer."

"He's a bit old for a rock star," Nadja said with a smile.

"Oh, he could still be one of those. These days, it seems that some people are never too old to make a comeback."

"You don't mean that, do you? Somehow, I can't see

him as a rock star," Nadja responded, trying to conjure up an image of Franco on stage with a microphone.

"No, I'm joking. He could have been an opera singer. All right, he wouldn't have made it to the Scala, except as a reserve member of the chorus. But he could have, in the past tense, sung in one of the provincial opera companies. You should ask him to sing for you one day."

"I only know one aria," Franco chimed in, "from *Rigoletto*. Piero knows which one. Don't you, Piero?"

"Of course, it's one of my favourites too. I whistle it all the time," Piero replied, turning down his lips.

"If it's the one I'm thinking of then it's not among my favourites," said Nadja. "I'll ask him to sing something else. I don't know what. But it would have to be a more cheerful song – the sort you can dance to."

"Operetta then, not opera?"

"Yes. Culture with fun."

Turning the corner into the square, they came across Alessandro Galgano, who was standing motionless in a pose reminiscent of the Mad Hatter staring at his fob watch.

"Ah, Alessandro, what a surprise! I just mentioned your name to Franco and his friend here, Nadja," said Piero.

"Nothing bad, I hope. Oh, I'm sorry. Did Piero say your name's Nadja?" Alessandro asked, taking her hand and lowering his head to kiss it.

"Yes. It's short for Nadezhda," said Nadja, smiling but without showing her teeth.

"That's Russian, isn't it?" Alessandro asked.

"Knowledgeable, isn't he?" Piero said, laughing. "How did you know that, my old friend?"

"Must have picked it up when I was reading about the Russian Revolution once upon a time," Alessandro replied, with mock modesty.

"That must have been an exceptionally long time ago," quipped Franco, "when you were almost one of us."

"Before I grew up, you mean," retorted Alessandro, giving Franco a glum look.

"Now, now, you two," said Piero, wishing to preserve the bonhomie between his two friends, with whose capacity for competitive repartee he was very familiar. "Look, Alessandro, these two have to be off and, as I've said to them, I've got my captain's duties to perform. But why don't you and I have a bite to eat later on?"

"That's a great idea. Come around to my place. I've got some nice things in for supper," Alessandro said with a sweeping wave of his arm, alluding to his own generosity which, in his view, could easily match Piero's.

⋆

That evening, Franco and Nadja took a minor road along the coast to an isolated *merenderia,* known for its own farm-produced wild boar carpaccio, crumbly pecorino cheese and crostini. They chatted about the idea behind Franco's design and decoration of the canvas wall, which had featured prominently in the judges' decision to award one of the top prizes to the three girls to whom Franco had tacitly agreed to act as mentor. His relationship to Silvia was never broached.

Nadja remarked that Piero seemed kind-hearted and good-natured, although she thought that calling his son Midas was rather incronguous, even narcissistic. "Well, I bet that, over the years, quite a few people will have thought it perverse for someone whose profession is to design and make artefacts from this precious metal to call his son Midas, after the mythical king whose touch was said to turn all things to gold. Do you think that he might have had a conscious or unconscious wish for his offspring to follow in his footsteps? Another question to which I'd like an answer is: did his wife have any say in the choice of name for her son?"

"Ha, ha, that's funny. It's a good question. I've no idea. I only met her a handful of times. My guess is that she wouldn't have objected that much because, unlike Piero, she's quite rich. I've heard people say that her wealth was the main reason he married her. He certainly didn't do so because of her looks. I don't want to sound spiteful or uncharitable, but she has a beaky nose, bulging, bulbous eyes and scraggly hair. She inherited a laundry which she expanded and turned into a successful business, with shops and laundrettes all over Piemonte. That's the source of her wealth. She and Piero don't get on that well. That I can testify to.

"From the table talk I've had with the two of them – a couple of times at the beach and once around a supper table – she struck me as rather dull and narrow-minded.

In fact, she's the opposite to her jaunty, extrovert husband. And so, with regard to your original question, she's clearly got a good feel for numbers and therefore it might be that she's the one with the Midas touch, which she hopes her son will inherit."

"From what you've said, it sounds to me as if she's the one who might have come up with the name. If that's the case, then she has a sense of humour and intelligence that you didn't spot," Nadja said, narrowing her eyes and grinning.

"True, but getting back to Piero. He'd be the first to admit that he can come across as vain and a bit of a show-off," Franco said. Then he added in defence of his friend: "But looking at his good side, I can assure you that, as you noticed, he's an immensely warm-hearted person, and at times a tremendously generous one too."

"Yes, that's just how he came across to me. Do you know what?"

"No."

"It occurs to me that, since he's a goldsmith, choosing Midas as a name could indicate that he has a strong sense of self-parody. Therefore, perhaps he came up with the name for one reason, and his wife thoroughly agreed on the idea but for a completely different one. Even so, putting aside the reasons behind their choice, I bet that quite a few people say that parents who give their child that particular name are more than just a bit conceited and boastful."

"I'd say it could be a bit of all these things. One day, I might ask them. Well, Piero, at least. One thing

I'm pretty clear about, though, is that we should never underestimate the importance that parents attach to the names they decide to give their children. Sometimes, children actually derive benefits from their parents' choice. On the other hand, a person can really suffer, firstly as a child, and then as an adult, from the name they were given. What baffles me is that so few people change them," Franco said, stabbing at the remaining sliver of meat. Wanting to move on from Piero, he asked: "What did you think of Alessandro?" hoping to receive more of an amusing anatomical sketch than a dissection of his character.

"I can't say that I had much of a chance to form an opinion. A first impression? He's rather proper, I imagine. A conservative with both a small and a capital 'c'. Did Piero say his surname was Galgano?"

"Yes. He owns that large campsite we passed. He comes from an 'old family', as they say. It was well-to-do before the war. Still moderately rich, in fact, and with buckets of political influence, though not so much locally."

"Alessandro Galgano. The name rings a bell," Nadja said, puckering up her nose.

"Alessandro or Galgano?" Franco asked.

"Galgano. My father used to mention the Galgano family when he had friends around and they talked politics. They used to link his name with another man. Hmm, could it be someone called Donegani?"

"Could be," Franco said, hunching his shoulders. "Both Galgano and Donegani held high-ranking positions in the Fascist Party. The Galgano they might have been talking about was Ennio, who was Alessandro's uncle. The big difference between the two of them – Galgano and Donegani – was that whereas Donegani's money came from manufacturing, Galgano's wealth and status derived from owning lots of land."

"That's interesting, because my grandfather was a political prisoner before the war and had his smallholding confiscated," Nadja said, looking down.

"In that case, it could well have been one of the Galgano tribe or one of their buddies. They had a hand in the seizure of a huge number of farms from individuals whom they designated enemies of the people, including, perhaps, that of your grandfather," Franco said, visibly uncomfortable at the turn of the conversation.

Trampling across the broad contours of recent Italian history didn't bother him at all. In fact, it was one of his pleasures in life. He had already guessed, correctly, that he and Nadja read the same newspaper and in August went to the same *Festa de l'Unità* jamboree. What was making him uneasy was the fact that Nadja was still most definitely an outsider and in danger of transgressing the boundary onto the miry territory of the interlocking affairs of Montelorenzene families. However, since Franco hadn't indicated any desire to change the subject and she couldn't read his mind, Nadja pursued her train of thought.

"Yes, it was Donegani," she said. "Montecatini had been set up and run by the Donegani family, with Guido Donegani at its head. He was one of those who, early on, decided to tie his fortune to Mussolini. During the

1920s, he was often seen next to *il Duce,* decked out in his ludicrous fascist uniform. He really was right up there in the party system and in the end found himself president of the National Fascist Federation of Industries. At the end of the war, he was arrested as a collaborator."

For Franco, the word 'fascist' served as a theatrical prompt, urging him onto the stage to present a monologue drawn from his repertoire of historical events and the role of the personages involved. "Oh, no, don't tell me," he said, throwing up his arms. "Just like many other leading Fascists, he was arrested and then almost immediately set free. Is that what happened? I never understood what Togliatti was up to when he granted all those villains an amnesty. They were outright criminals, most of them murderers, indirectly if not directly."

"My father thought he was too timid to be the leader of the Communist Party," Nadja said, picking up a crust of bread to wipe up a remaining drop of oil on her plate.

"He was being magnanimous. The best that can be said about Palmiro Togliatti is that he was a bit of a coward," Franco added, feeling a need to defend the Party though not the person.

"I think that you're the one being charitable," Nadja said, with a mixture of anger and sadness. "However, whatever the truth, after the war the Fascists were soon back in government, under a new brand name, the Movimento Sociale Italiano. And when the party's leader, Giorgio Almirante, died a couple of years ago, guess who was prominent among the mourners. Yes, none other than Togliatti's widow."

"And who was his appointed heir?" Franco asked rhetorically. He was poised to answer his own question but noting Nadja's steady, intent look and her lip-tight mouth, he realised that he had interrupted her. He broke her gaze by looking down at his hands, which lay spread on the table like the paws of a sphinx. During the brief silence, he moved them onto his lap and looked up at her, smiling sheepishly.

"Where was I?" Nadja asked, leaning across towards him. "Oh, I remember. In the mid-1960s, Montecatini merged with the electricity company, Edison, to become Montedison," she said, biting her lower lip.

"You sound well informed about this company," Franco said, in a manner that was both a statement and a question.

"I am. And I ought to be. I worked there for six years, in the personnel department, which I think they're renaming 'human resources'. It's where I met my husband. He was a chemical engineer."

A cloud of hush briefly enveloped them.

"From what I can gather, Montedison behaved much the same as all large Italian firms," said Franco, climbing back into the ring. "How did Ferruzzi Finanziaria get involved in it?"

"In the late eighties, Ferfin, as it was known, built up a forty per cent stake in Montedison, ousted its chairman and created one of the largest agro-industrial groups in the world."

"Ah, some of this comes back to me," said Franco, suddenly deciding to invert his stock of information into a question. "Didn't the Ferfin-Montedison empire nearly collapse because it had accumulated massive debts?"

"It's my turn to be impressed, Franco," Nadja said, with a touch of surprise. "I can imagine that since you've lived here all your life and your brother is the mayor, you have your finger on the pulse of the largest employer in the whole area. But this level of detail?"

"Well, yes. We do our best to keep up to date with what's going on inside that Dante's inferno. But not only us. The *comune* does too. After all, the town does benefit from the fact that the company's located in our area. Apart from being a major employer, it's also a supporter of several of our social programmes, including the library. But eh, come on, in all honesty I certainly don't know nearly as much about its history as you do," Franco said, bowing his head in recognition of her evident mastery of the subject.

"I should know a lot. Not only did I work for Montedison, but so did my father. And when Donegani was released without prosecution, my father was a prominent member of the works' shop floor committee, which brought the workers out on strike in protest at the leniency shown to him by the courts. Of course, although the strike had massive support, it changed nothing. Donegani remained free. Fortunately, he didn't live long. One Monday morning, he was whisked away from this world with a heart attack."

"Not from a broken heart?" Franco said jokingly before adopting a more sombre look, unsure of how to position himself along the humorous-serious continuum.

"No fear of that," responded Nadja. "That only happens to nice people. He had a heart of steel, which over time became corroded by his own industry."

Franco nodded his agreement and, digging into his bulging bag of knowledge of the period, pulled out what had at the time been a much-publicised fact. "In 1945, such was Donegani's standing on the international stage that when he invited Churchill to stay with him for a couple of weeks at his villa on Lake Como, the British prime minister accepted, even though he knew full well that his host still stood accused of war crimes."

"Really? Britain's great hero did that?"

"You mustn't forget that Churchill was at that time totally committed and determined to return Italy to its pre-Mussolini state at any price, in order to keep the socialists and communists out of government."

"Now, I didn't know that either. That's much the same as happened to Vittorio Valetta, who was the managing director of Fiat during the war. In April 1945, when the partisans went to arrest him in Turin for collaborating with the Germans, who did they find in his villa?"

"Same story?"

"Of course. Standing next to the window was an English officer with a safe-conduct pass for Valetta in his hand."

By now, they had finished their desserts and declined a coffee, and it was Franco who looked at his watch first and proposed that they should think about leaving. For both Nadja and Franco, the week ahead was a busy one and so they agreed to meet again the following Sunday. On the Wednesday, he received a letter from her.

Dear Franco,

Thank you for a wonderful weekend. I hope that you enjoyed meeting up with Piero before he went back to Turin, and that you gave him my regards. It was also interesting to meet Alessandro Galgano. The name Galgano has helped me to refocus my attention on subjects which used to be so important to me.

I decided to have a bit of a clear-out at home, starting with piles of old papers on Montecatini and its successor companies, which I had amassed with the intention of one day turning the material into a short critical history of the company. It begins with the firm's origins in the late nineteenth century as a copper mining operation in the Pisa region through to its becoming Italy's largest chemical company early in the twentieth. My story ends in the sixties with its merger with Edison, the oldest Italian enterprise in the energy sector, to form Montedison.

The enormous profits and equally enormous losses made by the conglomerate and the financial and political scandals surrounding its activities all make for a fascinating tale. As you're the librarian, I thought that if I sent you a summary, you'd be able to judge whether a shorter account of the company's history would be suitable for inclusion in the Montelorenzo Library Newsletter. After all, given the company's plan to make so many local people redundant, the story could be of topical interest. We could talk about it when we meet on the weekend.

If you're wondering why I had built up such an archive on Montedison and bombarded you with all that information about the company's history when we were out enjoying a supper together, the reason is simple: as I explained to you the other day, my dad was an active trade unionist at its chemical plant near Montelorenzo. Apart from his prominent role in the Donegani affair, he was one of the leaders behind several industrial actions over the dangerous levels of toxicity in which the employees had to work, not to mention the lousy wages paid by the company. He fell seriously ill when he was just forty-nine and died quite horribly two days before his fiftieth birthday. The company refused to accept any responsibility for his death or pay any indemnity to my aunt, who became my guardian and looked after me. There's more to it, but in a nutshell that's what lies behind my interest.

Looking forward to seeing you on Sunday.

All my love,
Nadja

⋆

The following Sunday, Nadja, wearing a pair of green and white striped shorts, climbed onto the throbbing Guzzi, wrapped her arms around Franco's waist and they headed off to the beach. Afterwards, he took her back to Montelorenzo and gave her a tour of the library. They repeated the outing a week later and he showed her the proofs of the next Montelorenzo newsletter, which contained her article on Montedison. Nadja turned to face Franco, put her arms around his waist, pulled him in towards her and pushed the small hard bump of her belly into his. She held him there and gave him a prolonged deep kiss. She instinctively knew that the man she was holding was the one with whom she wanted to make love.

Until now, it had been Franco who had made the amorous physical advances. All of them tentative: the casual kiss of the cheek when they met and the kiss on her lips when they parted; the arm around her shoulder or dangled down over her hip but not touching her firm buttocks, which proportionately matched her small breasts. Although she was quite touched by his hesitancy – largely because of its novelty compared with her other male encounters – too much timidity and diffidence on his part had in the past dampened her sexual arousal. She knew that now was the moment to change the pace of their progress towards her sexual fulfilment and that it was going to be left to her to shift them into a higher gear.

When Franco suggested they go to his studio flat to see his paintings, she gave an irrepressible short gasp, kissed and hugged him again, took his hand and led him in the direction of where he lived, a place that had been pointed out to her but never visited. Once indoors and visibly panting, it was her uncontrollable surge of passion for her soon-to-be lover that compelled her to take command of the situation. She took off her shirt and quickly unclasped her bra. As Franco reached out to touch the erect nipples protruding from her large dark areolae, she unbuttoned his shirt, threw it across the room and pushed him onto the bed.

Minutes before midnight, they took tired time out to go to a popular bakery at a road junction where they bought and ate freshly baked brioche, laughed and ran along the pine-fringed beach. Afterwards, they returned to their sheets where Nadja squeezed Franco's hand at the sight of the tell-tale stains of their mutual lust. They spent most of the late summer together, finding no time for their friends and behaving like teenagers in their public displays of affection – though never in the town, where they were very rarely seen together. Franco sensed that for his part this was not another infatuation, while Nadja knew that this was a wholly novel experience, since she had a benchmark against which to compare the present.

⋆

She had been twenty-one when her friends and those of a young male engineer from Genoa, Fabrizio, had over-romanticised what was no more than an ordinary workplace liaison. While she'd had her doubts (as perhaps had he), their relationship was submerged under the weight of its idealisation by others. The predictable outcome of this peer group fantasy was that each of them led the other up the garden path to a wedding in a castle where she changed her status from girlfriend to wife. In retrospect, the only thing that she could unequivocally say that she and her husband shared during her eight faithful but unhappy years of marriage was the same employer. Later, during the post-mortem following their separation, she was the first to admit that she could never place her hand on her heart and declare that she'd thrown herself into the marriage, for the simple reason that she couldn't see what it was that she was supposed to throw herself into.

The period since her divorce had not been one of unbridled licentiousness, and the scant amount of sex she'd had during that time she would not describe as in any way memorable. More importantly for her, she had not met and spent time with a man with whom she felt she had much in common. There were only two things that she could truthfully say she felt passionate about: music was one and politics the other. Although she still hadn't heard Franco sing, and they had not listened to any music together, Nadja knew that they sang from broadly the same political hymn book and tingled with the thought that they were splendidly in tune.

★

It was in the second week of September that Nadja decided to go to the town's main bookshop. Once, she used to drop in quite regularly, but this was her first visit since she had passed the obligatory examinations allowing her to advance up the financial services' ladder. The sky had been overcast all day and she had no doubt that heavy rain could be expected to follow the first peal of thunder. Despite the threat of a downpour, she stuck to her plan and hurried to the shop in order to find a book that might help her to deal with all her confused feelings about that mysterious, amorphous, indefinable feeling called love. She was in no hurry and browsed casually, willing the sort of book that she vaguely had in mind to mysteriously jump off the shelf into her hands. She ventured inside the covers of several books whose titles intrigued her but, while two of them sparked her tinder-like desires, none quite fitted the bill.

After a while, she decided to turn to the bookseller for assistance. The owner, a bibliophile, quickly selected a handful of books from different sections in the shop, among which was Erich Fromm's *The Art of Loving*, which she quickly scanned, bought, took home, perused and finished over three evenings. She found its contents and theses convincing and reassuring and repeated the message that she had secretly been seeking: in a relationship founded on love, a person encounters something valuable and almost mystical that lies outside the ego. She found totally persuasive its underlying premise that over a lifetime the individuals involved regard each other as lovers and as best friends, nourishing one another in their individual and joint creative projects.

Yes, she said to herself, *Fromm is correct: love is the only reason for our existence, for it is love that gives life meaning. And, yes, we should make every effort to walk hand in hand with the same ideas, yet, at the same time, be ourselves, take responsibility for our personal growth and, as Father had wished, preserve our individual integrity*. As she read, she was reminded of her attentive, sensitive and gentle lover, who never, even in the most ecstatic moments of lovemaking, expressed a desire for her to have his child. It was this virtue above all others that underpinned her newly found contentment; it was the best antidote to her debilitating, sometimes painful, obsession. It was while in this frame of mind that she began to fantasise that she might really be Franco's Hope and at the same time his Venus, emerging from Botticelli's scallop shell. Taken together, these thoughts induced in her a mood of moderate optimism – a disposition that, to be truthful, was essentially foreign to her nature.

Having thoroughly approved of what she had read, she placed the book beside the Bialetti pot on the shelf above the table in her kitchen where, because he was spending so much of his free time with her, he would not only be bound to see it but be curious enough to peer inside. He took the bait, nibbled at it when she wasn't around and, afterwards, replaced it so carefully that she wouldn't know that he had been quietly sipping Fromm's magical (or delusional) potion. It was the notion of love as an art that particularly appealed to

Franco, because for him practitioners of any art – music, carpentry, painting or engineering – had to dedicate themselves to their craft and devote energy and thought to their creative activity. One day, the book vanished, but by then its contents, though never discussed, had been absorbed into their lives.

Up to this point in his life, Franco had always lived at home where, until very recently, virtually all his material requirements had been taken care of. Even as a student, he had basically lived at home, commuting to university and dossing down in the flats of friends when necessary. As a result, his knowledge of housekeeping was minimal. All his financial transactions were conducted through the post office, where he kept his savings. After consulting his sister and worldly-wise cousin, he opened an account at the bank where Nadja worked and set up three direct debits to contribute towards Nadja's household costs.

Once Nadja's aunt had established that Franco was more than a fleeting presence in her niece's life, she retreated into her own private space in the flat, but not for long. Despite Nadja's heartfelt appeals to her to carry on living with them, she returned without fuss to the village. She promised to drop in on them whenever she visited the hospital and she kept her word. However, barely three months after her departure for the village, she moved on to the cemetery.

★

Having completed his first-thing-in-the-morning office routine, which included reading from cover to cover one local and one national newspaper, Franco linked his fingers behind his head and gazed at the ceiling. He held the position for a minute or two, rolling his head in agreement with whatever he happened to be ruminating over, then suddenly made a totally out-of-character dash towards the library entrance, put up his note informing the world that he would be back in an hour and walked the short distance to Signor Galgano's house. He rang the bell and Alessandro came down to answer.

"Francesco, this is a surprise. Come in, my boy. I'm just finishing the newspaper. What do you think of this turn of events in the legal case being brought against the prime minister? No, don't tell me. It's way too early in the day for that political guff. I don't know about you, but the verbiage that politicians spill out is unbelievable. It's bad for the digestion, especially around breakfast time. So, how can I help you?"

"I'm not here about the campsite, I'm afraid. Well, not directly," Franco said, almost apologetically.

"Ah, I've been hoping that you'd come around to see me about that at some point. I've got through the summer without them doing anything, but it's like the proverbial sword of…" Alessandro closed his eyes and turned his head to heaven. "What's his name, for god's sake?"

"Damocles."

"Ah, yes, that's the one. Thank you. So, what do you mean by 'not directly'?"

"It's about the Montedison factory, actually," Franco said, looking as awkward as he felt.

"Yes, well, what about it?" Alessandro said, his lower lip drooping and quivering – a behavioural tic once diagnosed as a symptom of Tourette's syndrome. The triggering of his tic in this instance signalled that his brain at some level was registering that Franco seemed ill at ease. "You know I've never liked that factory and its hideous chimney. That's putting it mildly. In fact, I hate the bloody monstrosity. But you and the *comune* have never brooked any criticism of its presence because it meets the council's sole criterion of acceptability."

"Which is?"

"It provides jobs."

"That's true, and I accept and congratulate you for being so admirably consistent in your disapproval of the company's presence on our doorstep."

"Not disapproval but condemnation!" Alessandro said, wagging his finger at Franco.

"Fair enough. It's true that you've stuck your neck out a number of times over issues involving this company. I remember very well the occasions when you have accused the administration of not using its legal powers to impede, if not prevent, the company's owners from expanding on our territory, as it certainly has done over the years."

"Thank you. But I would like to add that not only did the council *not* use its legal powers to make it more difficult, but it did all it could to make it easier for the company," Alessandro said, and then stopped talking.

Both men recognised that the elder of the two had won this quick shoot-out between Morality and Facticity and that it was time to call it a day. “I’m sorry, Franco, I’ve got lost. You brought up the name of Montedison and wanted to say something.”

“Yes. The reason I’ve dropped in unannounced, as it were, is that a couple of days ago I was given a document which confirms everything that you have been arguing for such a long time. It chronicles the history of Montedison from the day it arrived in the area and lays out in detail the health risks its factory presents to the workforce and the harm it does to the environment,” Franco said, looking Alessandro straight in the eye.

Alessandro smiled and, tapping Franco’s shoulder, said, “You know those words are music to my ears. But, tell me, what are you going to do with this information?”

“Well, I thought that I’d begin by publishing it as a supplement to the library’s quarterly newsletter. Having been through it thoroughly and cross-checked the more astounding facts it cites, I’ve come around to thinking that the local population should be properly informed about the implications any further expansion the factory owners might have in mind will have for the community. I’m sure you’ll agree that the council would have to pay attention to any objections members of the electorate might raise.”

“We’re all democrats when it suits us, aren’t we?” Alessandro said, poking the air with an unclenched fist.

Conscious and annoyed that he had truly wrong-footed himself, Franco refrained from responding to the jibe and instead said hesitantly: "This brings me to the reason I'm here."

Before he could elaborate, Alessandro leapt in: "Hold on a minute. You just used the word 'expansion'. I thought the firm was planning to reduce its workforce."

"So did I, because that's what the newspapers have been telling us," Franco said, jiggling his shoulders. "To be frank, we both know that this is typical Montedison behaviour. The newspapers print what the company wants us to believe, while they quietly do the opposite."

Alessandro frowned but decided that he didn't want to continue that particular conversation. Instead, he asked: "So, Franco, why have you dropped in to see me? It must be important."

"Not really. We, Nadja and I, that is, were simply wondering whether you'd like to have supper with us one evening around at her place. If you have time, that is."

"Of course I have time! I'd be delighted to see your… er…girlfriend again. But listen, I was going to come and see you this morning, because I've had a call from Piero, who's coming down here for a few days and he's invited you, me and Nadja to supper at Il Piccolo Mondo. He'd like to know if we could all make it Wednesday week before he returns to Turin on the Friday. The three of us – you, Nadja and me – could get together some other time. Seeing Nadja twice would be better than seeing her once, and a decent space between the two occasions will prolong the euphoric torment, if you know what I mean," Alessandro said, in his characteristically effusive manner.

"That sounds good. I'm sure that I don't have

anything else on that evening, or any other evening come to that," Franco replied, as he tried to disambiguate what Alessandro could mean by euphoric torment. "I'll check with Nadja, but unless you hear from me by the end of the day, would you mind going ahead and telling Piero that Wednesday will be fine for the two of us? And, as you say, we three can meet some other time." Franco was as delighted by his reprieve as he was by Piero's invitation.

"I did mean euphoric torment, didn't I?"

"I don't know, but that's what you said: suffering from too much pleasure or something like that. That sounds like you all right. Don't worry. I can imagine what it is that you want to say."

"Good on both accounts. So, we're agreed then. Incidentally, what was the other thing you came to see me about?" asked Alessandro.

"Oh, that can wait." Franco smiled, adding enigmatically as he unfolded the scroll he was holding and handed it to Alessandro, "This is the draft of a piece that Nadja has submitted for publication as a supplement to our newsletter, which is already with the printers. She asked me to tell you that she would greatly appreciate your opinion on what she's written because she's heard from different sources that you're the best authority on the topic. As you can imagine, the sooner we receive your comments the better so that I can get it printed and circulated well before we meet up with Piero."

"Is this the interesting document you said you came across?" Alessandro said with a wink as he glanced at the title page of the typescript.

★

When Franco and Nadja arrived for supper with Alessandro and Piero at twilight, under a calm and virtually cloudless sky, it was still warm enough for a short-sleeved shirt and a sleeveless dress. Knowing that it could be chilly by the time they left, Franco had swung a lightweight cotton sweater over his shoulders and Nadja carried a silk wrap across her arm. The sea softly swished the sand on the beach and gurgled around the latticed limpet-encrusted metal pillars that supported a short pier, at the end of which was a dome with a framework of glass, metal and wood. Inside was Il Piccolo Mondo restaurant, and nothing else. A kilometre along the coast and out of sight, hidden by a belt of pine trees, was the spot where a subsidiary of Montedison disposed of its red gypsum effluent.

As it was off-season, the restaurant rarely had more than a handful of customers, except for the occasional birthday, name day or some other celebratory event. But while only a handful of the tables arranged irregularly around a dance floor were occupied and no band or any other music was playing, all the tables were nonetheless draped in heavy white linen, as if the management were anticipating the room to suddenly be magically invaded by crew and cast for a remake of Fellini's *Amarcord*.

Alessandro and Piero were standing next to a table by the window at the furthest point from the restaurant entrance, talking and laughing at the same time. Franco, relaxed but cautious, and Nadja, excited but nervous, joined them. Following the usual pleasantries, the three men laughed and joked as old friends do, while Nadja looked on. They remained standing long enough to give Piero time to finish one of his shaggy-dog stories. Then their host guided Nadja to her chair and they all sat down. After the waiter had come to the table for a second time and been waved away, they fell silent and studied the menus.

"Do you know what I recommend?" asked Piero. "And remember, this is on me."

"Oh no," the two other men objected out of courtesy.

"I insist. I invited you here," Piero said, like the gallant *Capitano del Popolo* he regarded himself to be. "I recommend you choose from the fish menu, but to start..." He went through each antipasto and then the pastas before commenting on the individual fish dishes. "You know what I like about this place?" he asked, smiling at each person in turn.

"The fish?" suggested Alessandro. Piero shook his head.

"It must be the pasta," Franco said, pointing at Piero. "Just look at him."

"You can talk, Franco. I've never seen anyone eat as much spaghetti as you," said Nadja brightly, before returning her eyes to the menu.

"No. I'm sorry but you're all wrong," said Piero, turning his head to look at the ceiling. "The food suits my palate and my pocket. In my opinion, the restaurant is above average but not wonderful. I shouldn't be saying that, should I, since I'm the one who chose the place?"

There was a brief silence. While Alessandro inhaled deeply and remained silent, Franco, puffing out his cheeks, had another guess. "All right, it must be that you like the restaurant itself?"

"Its setting?" Alessandro suggested, scratching his ear.

"Yes, I like the restaurant. And yes, I like its location, and at this time of the year I also like its atmosphere." Piero paused again and then said, leaning forward over the round table, "What attracts me to this place most of all is its name! The Little World. We are sitting in what is, for the time being, *our* little world. Don't you think that's a wonderful thought?"

The three guests chortled each in their own inimitable way, and Alessandro lifted his glass in a silent tribute to Piero who, turning to Nadja, said in an earnest voice, "The first toast is to you, my dear, for your excellent article in the newsletter. It was a superb account of the rise and fall of one of Italy's largest and best-known companies. I remember how, in the wake of an infamous scandal, there was a tremendous kerfuffle in the media and in Parliament, which culminated in the company falling from grace among the powerful. Just like that." Piero snapped his fingers and continued: "You have provided us with a riveting account, based on irrefutable facts, of the largest employer in the area. Your dissection of the company and the scoundrels who have sat on its board over the years was such a revelation. Words fail me – something which everyone here will tell you is unheard of. Yes, a brilliant piece of investigative journalism. And the way you told the story made it a gripping read. Do you know what? We should publish it as a separate pamphlet so that it reaches a wider public."

Franco's lips parted and his eyebrows lifted synchronously.

"Hear, hear," Alessandro said in a booming voice. Given his garrulity, he would have said more, but it was clear that *il capitano* did not want to relinquish the floor. Instead, squinting at Alessandro, Piero moved his hand up and down slowly, like the conductor of an orchestra, and resumed his flow. "The scandals and incompetence at the very top of industry and banking are astounding. We all know that. But the machinations of the leadership of this one company, so eloquently documented in Nadja's exposé, leave me speechless."

"I agree. What you have disclosed has opened my eyes like never before. These latest disclosures are beyond belief," added Alessandro.

"'Beyond belief'"? 'Never before'? 'Speechless'? I'm not sure about that. Nothing that happens in this country ever leaves anyone that I know speechless," said Franco. "Everything that Nadja wrote about the behaviour of our post-war prime ministers and the country's so-called captains of industry is all too credible."

"Oh, come on, Franco. It's not only in Italy. There's not a single European country – let alone the rest of the world – which doesn't have major financial scandals associated with politicians and businesspeople, not to mention footballers and all sorts of other celebrities," Alessandro interposed.

"If I may finish," Piero said, stroking the end of

his beard, "we often talk of the bribery and downright corruption among these 'captains' as though it's a new phenomenon. But did you know that even Dante, the great Dante Alighieri, was exiled from his native Florence for embezzlement and corruption?"

"Oh, Piero, please! You know the charges against him were groundless," Alessandro interrupted.

"Well, perhaps. Who knows? My point is that even the most celebrated, lauded and, eh, respected individuals, both past and present, have accepted favours and in one way or another abused their position at some point in their lives. In my opinion – and let me say, by 'my opinion', what I mean is the opinion of a person who is both reasonably well informed and, at the same time, the ordinary man in the street – it's those at the very pinnacle of our society who are the most contemptible!" Piero ended, knocking the table with his knuckle.

"It's not just those at the very top," Alessandro said with feeling, rolling his head.

"Come on now, Alessandro," Piero said slowly, "you can't compare them," he pointed up to the domed roof, "with those at the bottom, who from time to time – how shall I put it? – break or bend the rules in order to do someone or themselves a favour. As an impoverished *Capitano del Popolo*, I solemnly declare that diners in this Piccolo Mondo, diners such as us, are light years away from them," again pointing upwards, as though to the ceiling of the Sistine Chapel for divine confirmation. "The newspaper and media magnates and moguls and their banking friends who finance them – with our money, don't forget – and the politicians who—"

"Do you mean that the big fish in the small sea don't count for so much?" Nadja asked mildly. "Because if you do, then I'm sorry to say that I disagree, because those fraudulent, deceitful, diminutive fish, those minnows, which would be lost and gobbled up in the big lakes and seas, swim and survive very well in their protected crystal-clear ponds and murky pools."

The table drifted into the equatorial doldrums as each of the men reflected on their own small worlds and how they managed to survive in them. Franco broke the silence by producing and then blowing a quick pip on a boatswain's whistle which, having once received it as a party gift, he always carried with him. He told the other crew members assembled in the Piccolo Mondo a funny story about the gross misconduct of which a leading member of the governing party in Rome had been accused. This prompted Alessandro to remember a bizarre incident involving a foreign family, who had stayed at his campsite the previous year. Piero, who had roared with laughter at both stories, then recounted a yarn of his own about a client who had commissioned him to design and produce a gold-plated goblet.

Rather than a normal chalice, he said, this client, who was called Gabriele, wanted him to solder a spear onto the handle, while its base would be the shape of a clam. Over the years, he'd regularly received requests that he considered extraordinarily odd, as most people would, but none had been as outlandish as this one.

The commission intrigued him to such a degree that he had spent hours in a Simenon-like search for clues that might help him to understand what could lie behind this client's eccentric specification.

It turned out that this Gabriele happened to suffer from a chronic illness which Piero had only come across once before, when it had been a woman who had exhibited analogous symptoms. He went on to regale them with an elaborate description of Gabriele's appearance, and of the enormous run-down, bougainvillea-smothered villa in which he lived and where he regularly entertained a weird selection of guests. The villa itself was a short distance from the ruins of a legendary abbey, nearby to which is a sword embedded up to its hilt in a stone. Bending over the table and swivelling his head, he recounted in a whispering voice three different events that he had attended at the villa, the most bizarre of which was the occasion when the invitees included a travelling troupe of the *commedia dell'arte*.

Count Gabriele, as he liked to be addressed, had commissioned these artistes to mime a story of their choice from Boccaccio's *Decameron*. Piero described in detail what he considered to be a brilliant interpretation of the book, beginning with a witty review of our human vices and concluding with a round of tragic love stories, all of which were somehow contrived to have happy endings. Piero stopped, stroked his beard and looked expectantly around the table for comments and questions, before adding: "It behoves me to say that Boccaccio would not be Boccaccio if he omitted to include in his cast Griselda, one of the key romantic characters in European literature."

"Forgive my usual ignorance, Piero, but who is this Griselda?" Alessandro bravely asked.

Piero smiled, cocked his head and gave a chuckle. "Franco knows, don't you, Franco?" Not wanting anyone to be embarrassed, Piero immediately answered his own question: "To put it bluntly, she is a character familiar to, and, I have to admit, rather resented by, the modern woman. Why? Because Griselda is known for… yes, her enduring patience and wifely obedience." He looked at Nadja and said with a wink: "It's all right, Nadja, Franco isn't at all demanding and, as you know, always expects everyone to be patient. And, why is that?"

Nadja smiled and replied: "Because his greatest vice has to be his timekeeping. As for obedience, I don't think that he ever expects that from anyone."

"Oh, I agree," said Piero, "he's too much of a democrat."

"Democrat, did you say? No, no! To go by my experience, he's more an anarchist than a straightforward democrat," Nadja said, slapping Franco's shoulder.

"Yes, no fears there for you, Nadja. But, if no one minds, could we please steer clear of the 'D' word," Alessandro pleaded, his hands clasped as though in prayer, thus neatly paving the way for Piero to change the subject. "Apropos the person mentioned during our post-prandial a few weeks ago, Franchino, do you remember the name of one of the stars in the film version of the *Decameron*?"

"Since Pasolini was the director, it must have been Ninetto Davoli," Franco said with a grin.

"Spot on, Franco. Did you actually see the film or is it that you remember me mentioning Davoli?" Piero asked, turning his eyes up before closing them for a couple of seconds, while at the same time moving his lips as if silently addressing a deity.

"Both. I did go to see it and how could I forget your comparison?"

"Please, Piero, come on. I don't care about Davoli ravioli. Finish your story. I'm intrigued to know why you went to so much trouble," Alessandro said.

"Fine. I'll tell you. First of all, though, let me make it quite clear that I wasn't afraid he might disapprove of me as a person. Nor was I worried that he might become disenchanted with what he had commissioned. No, what terrified me was that this capricious man might quibble about the size of the substantial fee that we had agreed, which as far as I was concerned had to cover more than just my artistic efforts. Over time, it struck me, and friends I consulted agreed, that the fee I was to receive should incorporate an element of financial compensation for my tireless, fawning sycophancy. That's why."

The audience coughed and clapped throughout Piero's account of his idiosyncratic client and his retinue, applauding both the anecdote and his uproariously theatrical narration of it.

"So there we are," Piero finished, putting his elbows on the table and tapping the tips of his fingers together.

"The way you tell your stories is one of the main reasons that year after year you're nominated to be *il capitano del popolo*," said Alessandro.

"I'm not sure about it being *the* main reason," Franco interjected, "but it's one of very many good reasons."

"Thank you very much, my friends," Piero responded, bowing his head.

Franco raised his glass as if he was going to propose a toast to the raconteur but instead said, "I'm fascinated to know what it was that this man suffered from. Was it a genetic illness? You know what they say about the link between aristocrats and inherited diseases."

"It could be genetic; after all, we now know that our inherited genes are responsible for many of our physical ailments and, eh, our mental disorders. However, what he had is unlikely to be inherited – though I certainly wouldn't discount that possibility. No, what this chap had was a medical condition known as satyriasis."

"What's that?" asked Alessandro.

"In medical terms, it refers to a condition described as excessive or uncontrollable sexual desire in a male," Piero said, with the calm air of a consultant talking to a patient whom he had diagnosed with the complaint, before offering him or her his commiserations or congratulations. "It's also known as hypersexuality or hypersexual disorder. But, if you don't mind, I'd rather not go into greater detail, least of all in the presence of a lady."

"Oh, I could not agree more," Alessandro was quick to declare with a sarcastic scowl. "However, I've a sort of subsidiary question. I'm fascinated to know, how do you describe a woman with these symptoms?"

"You call her a nymphomaniac. You know, women who are talked about as having an excessive appetite for sex," Nadja said, swivelling her eyes, tickled by the twist that the friendly exchange had taken. She had barely managed to suppress a chuckle when she noticed that Franco's face was beginning to redden. Emboldened by the way she'd been received into the company of the three men, by Piero's praise for her article in the newsletter (endorsed by Alessandro) and by the uninhibited flow of the conversation so far, she felt able to speak her mind and steer them back to the *terra firma* of politics – to a place where she intuited Franco would feel safer, away from the treacherous sea of sexual innuendo.

"Franco, going back to what we were talking about earlier, the trouble is that the Italian Communist Party, the Pee-Chee as we used to call it, and the Socialist Party were all part of the same stench given off by all our politicians regardless of their colour. Just reflect for one minute on the current president. Despite the fact that he used to be a member of the Pee-Chee, do you know what he did when the constitutional court put its foot down and refused to ratify the legislation designed to give Bermeloni immunity from prosecution? I'll tell you. He steps in, says that he 'can see no reason for delaying its passage into law' and immediately signs the bill," Nadja said, mimicking the old man's manner of speaking.

"I know, I know. And it gets worse," said Franco, raising his arms above his head, semaphoring the ineffectualness of the leadership on the left of the political spectrum.

"Yes, it does get worse, doesn't it? How many senior politicians on the Left denounced this cowardly, ignominious act? Not one!" said Nadja, wrinkling her mouth in an expression of despondency before touching and stroking Franco's arm consolingly. "To be fair, my dear, that's why millions of voters turned away from the Left."

"And voted for a new political party whose name escapes me," chimed in Piero, impishly.

"Don't worry. Franco will remind you what it's called, and he'll also explain why it's so successful," Alessandro said.

"Indeed, I shall," said Franco. "It's not that difficult to understand. First of all, by voting for a new party, people are telling the mainstream political parties that they're fed up with all of them. Secondly, this new party promises to do what everyone in the country wants, which is to give their word of honour to prosecute all those found guilty of involvement in illegal activities, with no one being above the law and able to claim exemption."

"So, what's wrong with that?" Alessandro challenged.

"Nothing's wrong with that at all. It's just that, unfortunately, as we all know, there will be people who, in spite of having unquestionably abused their positions and behaved dishonestly or amorally, will escape prosecution."

"Why is that?" Alessandro persisted.

"Frankly, because there are too many of them to prosecute. And those the courts do manage to prosecute, we can be sure, as sure as the fact that the best prosciutto comes from Parma, that they'll find clever, rhetorically brilliant, top-of-the-range Mercedes-driving lawyers to defend them and argue that 'they acted within the law'."

"That is, if you don't mind my saying, Franco, an instance of your wanting to achieve too much too soon. At least in this case, let's make a start. *Festina lente* is my motto." Alessandro paused and then changed gear, seemingly into reverse. His softly, softly voice that had lacked conviction now sounded like a haranguing populist politician: "That's why, as far as I'm concerned, people are quite right to take the risk and vote for a party whose politicians pledge to rid us of this ubiquitous putrefaction. What's more, I believe that those found guilty should not simply be denounced in the media but pilloried and humiliated and properly punished."

"Phew! I've never heard you talk like that before," Franco said, discernibly shocked by Alessandro's oratorical outburst. "On your morning constitutional today, did you take the road to Damascus by mistake? Or is this change a result of your meeting with Lombardi a few weeks ago?"

"Please, Franco, put Signor Cynic back into your pocket," Alessandro retaliated.

"I do apologise, Alessandro," Franco said, anxious not to offend, "but the trouble is that corruption can never be eradicated altogether. It's everywhere in one form or another. And, I regret to say, you can't change the way people think by diktat. Nor can you change the way they behave simply by employing more and more government inspectors to enforce the law."

"I wish I didn't agree, but what Franco has said is fundamentally true," Nadja said, tapping the table with her forefinger.

"That's very pessimistic, my dear. Leave the pessimism to the men, especially the older ones," Piero said, before characteristically raising his eyebrows. "The question is this: where do we start if we are to successfully bring about the changes everyone seems to want?"

"Right at the top," Franco said, clearing his throat. "We need to ask how it was possible for this man to climb to the pinnacle of the greasy political pole."

"There are so many theories floating about to explain the man and his empire, so you tell us, Franco," Piero said, inclining his head as a form of genuflection to the librarian's knowledge on the subject.

"All right. I'll be brief and begin with a question." Franco put his arms on the table, looked at each of them and asked, 'From whom did Bermeloni inherit his post as prime minister? I'll give you a clue. It wasn't his immediate predecessor."

Alessandro and Piero shook their heads and Nadja sat motionless. All three remained silent.

"Well, I'll tell you. Both Croce, the leader of the Socialist Party, and Bermeloni came from Milan. Two years after Croce's election to that post, Bermeloni established his first major television station. That's when their careers became entwined." Franco paused for dramatic effect then took off again: "Bermeloni was funded by loans from banks controlled by none other than the Socialist Party. And in this den of scoundrels, Bermeloni returned the favour by funding Croce's *personal* political machine."

Both Alessandro and Piero indicated their agreement by shaking their heads, affecting disbelief.

"Croce was godfather to Bermeloni's first child and, a few years later, there he was again, this time as best man at Bermeloni's wedding to the child's mother."

"It's astonishing! Words fail me. No they don't. Italy is a modern Greek tragedy," Piero interjected.

"Personally, I prefer Roman tragedies, and so should you. For one thing, they're closer to home," Alessandro added.

"Do you have a particular tragedy in mind?" Piero asked with a twinkle.

"Oh, stop it, you two," Nadja said crossly.

"Thank you, Nadja," Franco murmured, touching her foot gently. "And when Croce became prime minister, one of the first things he did was to pass a law—"

"Yes, it's coming back to me," Piero cried out, exultantly. "That particular law did nothing less than save Bermeloni's national television networks from being closed down."

"Absolutely," Franco said, taking back the reins. "These two men were the Castor and Pollux at the apex of Italian politics. How do you think Silvia Romano, Croce's mistress, managed to have such a dazzling career in state television?"

As he spoke, the normally placid librarian grew increasingly agitated. Aware that his raised voice was drawing glances from the occupied table nearest to them, Franco rubbed his neck and asked in almost a whisper, "Do you remember how much Croce was rewarded for his services?"

"No," said Nadja, in a conspiratorial tone, "but I heard that it was a huge sum."

"Our Socialist prime minister received the equivalent of ten million euros. And where did all this money go? Into his foreign bank account, naturally. Three years later, when the scale of Croce's corruption was exposed, he became the most execrated public figure in Italy."

At that, all three men compressed their lips and gave out loud puffs of air. Alessandro wrung his hands in *Schadenfreude* under the tablecloth, while Piero and Nadja shook their heads despairingly. After a brief pause, Franco inhaled deeply and delivered the best *coup de théâtre* ever enacted in Il Piccolo Mondo: "As Croce fled into exile to go and live in his villa near the ruins of the Antonine Baths on the outskirts of ancient Carthage, Bermeloni climbed onto the political stage to play his leading role in our Italian political farce."

"It's true," said Alessandro, delighted to endorse Franco's summary of the association between the two politicians, especially because of his deep loathing of Croce the Socialist.

"Indeed it is, I'm sorry to say. As we all know, the First Republic collapsed amidst an outburst of public outrage at the soaring national debt and above all the stratospheric levels of political corruption."

"May I add," Nadja interjected, "when we talk of

political corruption, what we must understand is that it extends far beyond the revolving presence of people associated with the Mafia in both government circles and the economy."

"Thank you, Nadja. Unfortunately, the hopes and dreams safety-pinned to the birth of the Second Republic were virtually suffocated in its cradle when at its head appeared *il cavaliere,* someone more corrupt than all the others." Having recovered and raised his political standard, the librarian now rode back on his chair and, with a sweep of his arm, invited the Greek chorus to chant their indignation.

"Togliatti, Croce, Bermeloni, Fini – what difference does it make?" Nadja asked dejectedly, tapping her glass with her people's blood-red varnished fingernail.

Now that they were sufficiently enraged, the four of them threw themselves exuberantly into the popular dinner party game of gossiping about the malfeasance of the country's excessively wealthy, of all and sundry in the political class, and everyone in a position of authority, with the spectre of the Vatican's role behind the scene in most things.

During dessert, they again took to exchanging tales, which were interspersed with a mixture of true and false facts and figures – all couched in the most extravagant terms – about a hotchpot of people with a prominent presence in the public arena, who they thought should be expelled from their posts, prosecuted and incarcerated.

By the time they reached coffee and limoncello (for Nadja) and grappa (for both Alessandro and Piero), they had begun their descent from politics at the planetary level to their own mundane *piccolo mondo* and found themselves hovering at a Google Earth position above Montelorenzo Scalo. At that height, above the cereal fields and the barber's pole chimney, they enjoyed a panoramic view of a sizeable territory where a contest was taking place between two contrasting industries: manufacturing, represented by Montedison, and tourism, represented by, among others, Alessandro Galgano's campsite, *Il Paradiso*.

"Alessandro," Franco said, leaning across the table, "I'd like to take you up on your point about the loss of jobs that will occur should your *bête noire*, Alberto Ferraro, go bust or simply shut down his campsite and leave. Your campsite, plus his, together with a dozen others in the area, will never create enough jobs to employ all those made redundant by Montedison."

"No, of course not, I know that," Alessandro said dismissively. He wasn't foolish enough to joust on terrain demarcated by such a crude fact.

Franco squinted and carried on. "It's just occurred to me that what people like you in the tourist industry want to do – and I don't mean you personally – is to make us go backwards and create a new peasantry. You know, you employ people on your campsite during the summer and when the last of the tourists have left, they are demoted to peasant status and trot off to harvest the land and then produce wine, olive oil and other local organically grown foodstuffs."

Alessandro said nothing. Franco hadn't yet said

enough for him to discern whether he was making a passing observation or whether this was an opening gambit foretelling an imminent full Puccini challenge.

"And," said Nadja, joining the flow, "those Montedison employees, who've been through higher education and now lost their jobs, well, they'll form small companies to process this produce. Then they will draw on the social capital they have been building up in anticipation of such stormy times ahead."

"I'm not quite sure what you mean by that," Alessandro said, pretending naivety.

"Of course you do, Alessandro. You would do exactly the same. You would start by phoning around to people you know in your various networks of family and friends to find outlets for your products. No doubt you do this in the case of the campsite service which you provide, not to mention the labour you need for your olive harvest," Nadja said quietly, with a pleading frown.

"It's not difficult to predict what will happen next," Piero added in a sober tone as he forked a small piece of orange polenta cake into his mouth. "Because they find themselves in a fiercely competitive market, these young, capable and creative entrepreneurs will be forced to do whatever they can to protect their outlets and networks." He paused and sucked in air and watched the faces of the other three commensals contort as they realised the terminal station to which the logic of this argument was heading.

"It seems to me, Franco," said Alessandro, in the soothingly avuncular way that he had recently come to adopt towards the librarian, "you acted very wisely when, although you had a university education, you chose to follow in your father's footsteps and become a cabinet maker."

"Such prescience. I told you, Nadja, Franco's an extremely talented person. Here's another instance. As Alessandro says, Franco's decision places him well and truly among the avant-garde who saw the direction in which the economic wind was blowing."

Despite the praise being heaped on Franco, Nadja could see that the flowing tide of words might again begin to turn against Franco. Her eyes moved from one man to the other and could see no malice on either of their faces. Even so, her limited knowledge of their individual backgrounds led her to conjure up an image of their coracle coasting casually towards the rocks marked *Franco's Discomfort*.

"The real problem is our overuse of fresh water," she said out of the blue. "Our rivers and aquifers are already hard-pressed to meet the ever-increasing demand for water even at the best of times, let alone when we have droughts, which are becoming more and more frequent."

The three men looked at her and said nothing. She had raised another profoundly serious question. Everyone was talking about water shortages. In order to break the silence, Nadja opened up her arms and hands, as in the pose often used by artists portraying martyred saints, and asked: "Do you know where the water companies have been getting their water from?" When no one answered – because they didn't know and wanted to avoid the embarrassment of guessing wrongly, she told them: "From deep wells on the coastal plain, which has meant that the pressure in the freshwater aquifers has fallen, and salt water has infiltrated the water table."

"And therefore?" Piero questioned.

"Quite simple. The water from aquifers has to be desalinated at a horrendous cost," Nadja said, and decided herself to dry up. With Alessandro and Piero sitting with firmly closed lips, it was left to Franco to fill the awkward, noiseless space and to readjust the balance on the board of words. "To be positive for a moment, desalination plants have to be manufactured, installed and maintained, thus creating more jobs, especially in the engineering sector, which can't be a bad thing."

"Fine. But it's the tourist industry which will provide most jobs directly and indirectly, including the demand for, yes, desalination plants," Alessandro said, pressing home his temporary advantage.

Franco and Piero looked at one another sceptically, but rather than set up a court to examine the flaws in Alessandro's case, Piero came up with a suggestion designed to satisfy everyone. "Nadja, why don't you write something about the ecological damage done around here by Montedison and other manufacturing companies? Franco could put it in the next issue of the library's newsletter. It would make a perfect follow-up to the last one."

"What a splendid idea," Alessandro exclaimed.

"I also think that's a brilliant bit of thinking, Piero. Bearing in mind that Nadja would be focusing on water shortages and examining who the main consumers are, the study might be extended to include the tourist industry," Franco added, making a bid to influence the remit of Nadja's investigation.

"That's absolutely fine by me," said Alessandro, feeling quite self-satisfied with the turn of the conversation.

"Unfortunately, Alessandro, we all know that increased beach tourism can't by itself provide work for all the people looking for jobs locally," Franco added, putting his hand across his mouth, implying that he felt obliged to stop talking, when, in fact, he had stopped because he had run out of things to say.

"Of course not. There are too many people trying to find a tiny spot on the beach to plant their parasols. And as Nadja has correctly pointed out, something has to be done to protect our coast which, incidentally, could be the basis for yet another article for our newsletter. So, what's the answer?" Alessandro paused for someone to provide an answer. "Oh, come on. It's staring you in the face." After waiting a longish minute for the tired minds beside him to come up with a solution to the riddle he had posed, he thumped the table and jubilantly declared, "The answer has to be – inland campsites like mine!" Franco gave a wan smile. Nadja touched his leg under the table and Piero threw back his head and gave a loud thunderclap of a guffaw, which served as a signal to them all to laugh and clap.

Each of them had played their predictable political card and placed it face up on the unblemished tablecloth, which was still as gleamingly white as any manufacturer of washing powder could wish to see in a television advertisement demonstrating the outcome of the use of their product. The evening had left each of them with a warm glow and a sense of contentment in the knowledge that, although none of them had come up with a solution to the serious topics they had touched upon, neither had anyone else in their *piccolo mondo* or in the big wide world. Piero called for the bill. They stood up, embraced, walked out of the restaurant and went their separate ways.

★

Because the sky's anti-cyclonic ultramarine blue carried a promise that the air would have a late autumnal chill, Franco had gone to the library early to light the wood-burning stove. He wanted to ensure that it would be warmer inside the building than in the homes of less well-off users, some of whom had originally seen and treated the library as a refuge. Because he, personally, knew the difference between having and not having books at home, Franco was quietly proud that the library opened new vistas to some of his fellow citizens who, having previously never read a book, now spent hours sitting immersed in fiction and non-fiction, borrowed books to take home and even submitted requests for books to be loaned from other libraries.

It was late afternoon and he was sitting at his desk, handwriting a letter. The wastepaper bin was full, yet the height of the piles of newspapers and magazines on his desk remained constant. Alessandro Galgano was looking down over his shoulder. The surface stillness of the Vermeer-like scene was ruffled as Costanza Veronese walked into the frame. She squeezed herself into a position behind Franco and bent over to see what the two men found so absorbing.

"You look like a couple of conspirators," she said with a laugh.

"We might be. Only I can't imagine what we might be conspiring about," Alessandro said, acting as their nominated spokesman.

"I can. Franco, I've just heard a rumour that's doing the rounds, and it's about you," Costanza said.

"Me?" Franco stopped writing and looked up, with his customary deadpan face.

"Oh, come on, Franco. Are you going to confirm or deny what's being said?"

Franco put his hand on his head, ruffled his hair and gave one of his typical Delphic replies: "You tell me what's being said then I can confirm or deny it."

"According to the rumour, you might be getting married. Are you?"

"Would you like a coffee?" Franco said in reply to his friend's reasonable question, which she had asked out of genuine concern, not curiosity.

"It depends on the answer to my question. You know I don't drink alcohol, but if the rumour is correct, I shall drink a glass of champagne."

Franco picked up the phone, called the bar and placed

an order for three glasses of prosecco. Then, turning to look Costanza in the eye, he gave a simple trisyllabic answer: "Probably."

Although Costanza's smile did not fade, what she said was edged with the faintest impatience. "What do you mean, 'probably'? Are you or aren't you?"

"Let's go and sit around the table over there. It'll be more comfortable and the drinks will be here in a couple of minutes."

"That's unlikely," muttered Alessandro. "It's Giorgio's day off, and you know what Carlo is like."

The three of them shuffled away from the cluttered desk to a table in an alcove, bare except for a small stack of un-reshelved books, which Franco pushed to one side with his elbow, allowing them to sit at arm's length from one another in order to ensure that each had sufficient space to gesticulate freely.

As they sat down, Franco turned to Costanza and said: "At this moment in time, the only answer that I can honestly give to you is yes, I think so."

Costanza's initial light-hearted tone slowly slid behind a cloud. "Oh, come on, Franco! 'Yes, I think so.' What sort of reply is that? We all know that you're an old ditherer, but getting married is a serious matter. Tell me, is it that young woman in Castiglione?"

Franco still said nothing, as though he had been struck dumb. Instead, he raised his eyebrows, thus repeating gesturally what he had already said.

"*Dio!* Your silence is truly deafening, Francesco Puccini. Do you want me to try to guess which of the three wise monkeys you're aping? Ha, ha." Costanza, though annoyed, couldn't stop herself from tittering at her own pun.

Since it was a constant hovering presence in Alessandro's own mind, he had regularly reminded Franco that his long-standing and close relationship to Costanza meant that it would be right and proper, and also politic, that she should hear what was supposed to be his big secret directly from him, not through the Montelorenzo grapevine. In fact, he had done his best to impress upon the librarian that it would be a gross mistake for him not to be the one to tell her.

Franco's stock response to these admonitions was that he could not agree more, and every time the matter popped up in conversation, he would thank Alessandro for reminding him and declare that he intended ringing her the next day or day after. He would then ostentatiously scribble 'Ring Costanza' on a yellow Post-it and place the message on the telephone. But he never did, on the grounds that he had changed his mind after having come to the conclusion that it would be much better to tell her in person when they met, which he was convinced would be quite soon.

However, unknown to him, she had for months been preoccupied with a new, long-distance romantic attachment, which had forced her to abandon many of her calendarial rituals, including regular visits to Montelorenzo. As a consequence, by the time the vague rumour, passed among the few that Franco was getting married, had percolated down to Costanza, it was widely circulating as general knowledge in the hilltop community.

Alessandro, guessing that Costanza must feel peeved for having been kept in the dark regarding the massive change about to occur in an old friend's life, began to fidget more than usual as he sent the quixotic part of his brain in search of a way to pull the carriage of chatter out of the rut in which it was becoming stuck. Weighing up the merits of interceding on Franco's behalf against the cost of annoying his campsite counsellor, Alessandro opted for pressing the jolly-up button.

"I'm sad to say, Costanza, but you're a bit out of touch with the excitement and turmoil of life down here. You can't imagine the things people get up to in Montelorenzo when you're not around. But then how can you possibly be up to date with everything that happens in this part of the world when you don't come down nearly as much as you used to, or as much as we'd all wish you would?" Alessandro gave Franco an undisguised conspiratorial wink, Costanza a tiny bow and himself a pat on the back for what he considered to be his neat and tactful intervention.

Costanza's reaction to Alessandro's ploy to deliver a heart-winning, wise fool's jest was the opposite to what he had anticipated, for his words had added to her accumulating sense of being the subject of deceit. Not a great deceit but a deceit nonetheless, which left her poised to tell him that she found his crude attempts at flattery juvenile and verging on the offensive. However, as she was only too aware of Alessandro's fondness for her, she refrained from saying anything so unkind and, in the circumstances, needlessly callous. Instead, she agreed with him; after all, it was quite true. She didn't come down to see them as often as she once did. Even so, she felt compelled to demonstrate to both of them that, despite her long absences, she remained in touch with goings-on in the town, such as births, deaths and marriages.

"What I'm interested in right now is far more important than the number of litres of olive oil the co-operative produced last year, or when the shop is going to close and whether it will ever open again," she said, before turning to look directly at Alessandro and, like a cross-examining magistrate, asking, "Have you ever seen this woman, Alessandro?"

"If I'm to be quite truthful, yes. I met her once. That was during last year's festival when Piero introduced me to her," Alessandro mumbled, having decided that it would be better not to mention the meal at Il Piccolo Mondo.

"What's her name? Someone said that she thought it was Nadja."

"Yes, it's Nadja," Franco said with a smile.

"Let me get this straight. You're going to get married to this Nadja. Now I know. Franco, that's terrific news! Come on, let's drink that prosecco that Carlo brought a moment ago." With that, she clapped her hands, laughed loudly, rose from her chair and, bending down over her hunched friend, threw her arms around his neck and gave him a prolonged hug. Then, pulling herself back, she asked: "Is it going to be a big event or a registry office job with one or two witnesses? And who's going to be best man? It can only be Antonio."

Franco put his arms behind his head and, suppressing a yawn, replied, "You're jumping the gun, Costanza. The date hasn't been fixed yet and no arrangements have been made."

"Why not?" asked Costanza.

"Because I haven't actually asked her whether she wants to marry me," Franco answered, pulling the sort of face that raises doubts about the sanity of the person posing the question. "However, I sort of expect her to accept my proposal. As to the number of people, well, I can tell you that it won't be many, just a small gathering. You and Alessandro are on the list, of course. As to your last question, no, it's not going to be Antonio. Fausto will be my best man. Though he may not be, because I haven't asked him yet."

Costanza rolled her eyes in astonishment and almost screamed his name. "Fausto? Fausto! That delinquent!" Alessandro Galgano's mouth dropped open; the choice reminded him of another tenuous and tangential link between the Puccinis and the Galganos in the Montelorenzene chainmail. In this case, the link was between Fausto and Alessandro's notorious uncle, Ennio Galgano, who many years ago had commissioned the young graduate architect to modernise his dilapidated family villa.

Franco took advantage of his stun gun declaration to ask whether one of them would mind holding the fort for ten minutes while he popped out to deal with the urgent matter to which Costanza had alluded.

"Someone else you've forgotten to tell?" Costanza asked.

"As a matter of fact, yes. I don't know why," Franco replied, his face reddening as his eyes flicked between them.

"I can't stay, I'm afraid," Alessandro said, assuming one of his set piece poses, in this case that of being a terribly busy man.

"All right, I'll wait," sighed Costanza, "but, Franco, I heard you say ten minutes – please, no more than twenty-five. It shouldn't take Alessandro here that long to tell me about the circumstances in which he was first introduced to Nadja. It shouldn't, should it, Alessandro?" she asked, ignoring what he had just said about having to rush off.

⋆

Franco left the library, crossed Piazza Garibaldi, descended a flight of steps and emerged in a narrow lane, Vico della Dispensa. He stopped at a house near the bottom and rang the bell. Without waiting for a reply, he opened its iron gate and entered a small courtyard. It was dotted with terracotta pots and urns, some plain, others with decorative designs, all varying in size and shape, and each filled with an evergreen plant or a cluster of seasonal flowers in bloom.

"Hello, Uncle, how are things? Is Fausto in?"

he asked an old man sitting in a chair, who raised his walking stick and pointed to a staircase leading up to a highly polished, panelled, chestnut door. Franco stood chatting for a couple of minutes then crossed the patio to the entrance of his cousin's house.

"Fausto, are you up there?"

"Yes," came the reply. "Sounds like you, Franco. Come on up."

Fausto's state-of-the-art open-plan accommodation was arranged vertically over four floors. A spiral staircase wound up from the ground floor – used for storing indoor and outdoor sporting equipment – to the first-floor architect's studio. Another open staircase led up to the bedroom, while a final flight led up to a bachelor-sized kitchen and living room where French windows opened onto a terrace large enough for a small table and two chairs. Here, one or two people could sit and watch the sun's daily journey from its rise over the hills and its setting over the sea. The house was designed for the comfort and convenience of one person, the owner, and to be an object of admiration for a transient bedroom guest.

"How are you? Haven't seen one another for ages," Fausto said cheerfully as they embraced.

"You're always off playing golf or sailing," said Franco, who wasn't in the least envious of his more affluent cousin's lifestyle. They had both grown up in the town, left to study at more or less the same time and returned to their birthplaces, which they had never felt the urge to leave again. They were children of their era, beneficiaries of the European post-war, social democratic, meritocratic ethos, which had offered their generation the opportunity to be both socially and geographically mobile. They had chosen to be geographically immobile and, of the two of them, only Fausto had decided to climb the social ladder.

"I hear you've got a new girlfriend," Fausto said with an unwitting snicker.

"I hear that about you every day." Franco ping-ponged back, adding, "I can see that you're getting ready to go out, so I don't want to take too much of your time."

Fausto smiled and shrugged.

"I've only dropped in to ask whether you'd be my best man."

"Franchino, you're not serious? I don't mean about asking me, but about your intention to marry!"

"Yes, just this once."

"You mean, just this once you're being serious, or just this once you're going to get married?"

"Both," said Franco.

"It's not that girl I saw you with in a place off the Aurelia in Cecisetta?" Fausto asked, sitting down on one of the two stools against the kitchen bar.

"Which *trattoria*? When?" Franco asked nervously, wondering who else might have seen him with Nadja. Ever since that first weekend at the town's annual summer festival, when they had been observed together, there had been nothing in the way their bodies spoke to one another for anyone to imagine that the person Franco was with was anything more than a casual female acquaintance, so rarely were they seen together. For reasons obscure even to himself, he had kept Nadja well clear of the town. Her visits were clandestine and during the quiet hours, when people were eating or sleeping. Only very much later did Franco look back and brood over why he had kept her concealed in the background, as though disavowing her.

"It was a few months ago. In Cecisetta, as I just said. It's an inconspicuous but popular place where I go to eat now and again when I'm in the area. How did you find out about it? Is it one of your new hangouts?" Fausto asked, spiking an olive in a small fish-shaped dish, which he then pushed across to his cousin.

"No." Franco shared his cousin's ability to see the amusing and absurd aspects of life, but not his extrovert character.

"No, what, Franco?"

"No, it's not one of my hangouts, as you put it."

"But yes, it was you in that *trattoria*? What's it called? Something like La Locanda dei Poeti?" Fausto volleyed. "If it was there, I can tell you exactly when I saw you. Listen, you must have read about the fire that destroyed a small factory in Castelovincenzo?"

"It would have been difficult not to have heard about it. Probably an accident funded by the Montedison management to distract attention from what they're up to."

"Franco, you haven't changed. Still the old conspiracy theorist. Anyway, I received a commission to be part of a team put together by a friend of the Galganos who lives in Livorno. It's a project to build a small gated condominium where the factory had been."

"Quite lucrative then?" Franco said with a smirk that

expressed his critical opinion of Fausto's involvement in such a scheme.

"Pays the bills, as they say. But listen, let me finish my story. One lunchtime, on my way back from a project meeting, I stopped off in Cecisetta to pick up a friend. It was when we drove past this place that I thought I saw you." While talking, Fausto picked up his desk diary and flipped through it.

"Here we are. Tuesday, the twenty-eighth of August. Saw Franco with woman in La Locanda dei Poeti in Cecisetta."

"You're joking," Franco said with a grin, marvelling at his cousin's meticulous attention to detail, which, together with his punctilious attitude to the way he dressed and his punctuality, went a long way to explaining his material and social success.

"No. I'm not joking. I was in Cecisetta on that day, and that's when I must have seen you."

"You didn't actually put that in your diary, though, did you?" Franco asked, wrinkling his forehead.

"I'm teasing. I *did* see you there, but no, come on, Franchino. Of course I didn't make a note of it in my diary. What I did do was to make a mental note that, contrary to what I've come to believe, you do sometimes wander well outside the *comune*. Seeing you with a woman I hadn't heard about was another first. Is that the one you're marrying?" Fausto queried.

"Yes." Franco's curt reply was intended to convey a hint of the irritation he was feeling towards his cousin's apparent indifference to the forthcoming event and, especially, to the way he referred to Nadja as: 'is that the one you're marrying'.

Fausto didn't respond for a few moments; instead, he pulled the olive dish towards him, targeted and swallowed, like a gecko, two olives, one green and one black, in quick succession, and then looked down at his folded hands. His studied stillness, following his violent jab at the olives, granted Franco time to read from Fausto's posture what his cousin felt about his news and request.

"I know what you're thinking," Franco said pre-emptively. "I never thought for a moment that she'd come up to your standards. Physically, I mean."

"It's often said that beauty is in the eye of the beholder and, like many adages, this one too is true."

"It is indeed. What I see on the outside is a distraction shielding the beauty within. I penetrated into the within before falling in love with the without," Franco said with a barely perceptible sigh, before nodding silently in his characteristic way, confirming to himself that what he had said was correct.

"Well put," Fausto said, chastened by Franco's pensive rebuke.

"As you'll find out, she can hold her own in conversation on a wide range of topics from literature and politics to down-to-earth small talk about your state-of-the-art kitchen fitments or surfboard. What's more, she's someone who is not afraid to express her opinions. And not just on current affairs and what's making the headlines. She's a person who, by any standard, would be described as being well read."

"You're a lucky man," Fausto murmured.

Franco's defensive description was accompanied by a slight narrowing of his eyes and a stern expression defying his cousin, who was staring at him mutely and expressionlessly, to say anything flippant or provocative. Fausto unconsciously inflated his nostrils and, sniffing the air, remained silent.

"Of all her virtues, there are two minor domestic ones which I think you'd appreciate," Franco continued. "First of all, she doesn't prattle on, or natter for the sake of it. Secondly, and best of all, she's not one of the world's grumblers."

"She sounds perfect," were the only words that Fausto could muster.

"Her main problem is that she's a bit of a worrier. If something makes her even slightly anxious then she begins to fret and becomes edgy," Franco said, holding up his hand, as if to say Halt!, intimating that this was his last word on Nadja as a subject to be described and explained.

"She's quite normal then," Fausto said matter-of-factly. "By the way, what is she called?"

"Nadja."

"Short for Nadezhda?"

"That's right. Well done, Fausto."

"Not difficult. That was the name of the wives of two of those men in our Pee-Chee pantheon. God, that was a long time ago."

"I thought that you had buried all your memories of those days."

"You're right. I have."

"Well, she's the person to help you dig them up again because, like her namesakes, nothing gives her more pleasure than a good political argument."

"I hope that she gains even greater pleasure from things other than politics. Whatever. You make it sound as though you've found a companion to help you face life's vagaries," Fausto said, displaying his uncertainty over whether his cousin had made a good choice. To his way of thinking, it was a bit early to look upon a lover as a companion.

"She's more than merely a companion, as you put it, and she definitely has more to offer than some of your girlfriends that you've introduced me to over the years. A couple of them really were right out of the bottom bimbo drawer," Franco said, and immediately wished he hadn't, for his statement had sounded more aggressive than he had intended.

"Eh, that's not fair. Come on, you know full well I've never been involved with anyone who could be called that, not even at the yacht club."

"How about the one who only talked about poodles and poltergeists?" Franco fired one last shot.

"All right, but Andrea was an exception. But now, seriously, let me say this. We – you and I that is – have so many things in common, yet we are quite different, opposite in fact, in one highly significant way. This one big difference has always been there. Do you know what it is?"

"Just one? Are you being serious?"

"Yes. I said 'one *big* difference'. Let me remind you. It's this: you have always lived in hope and now literally have hope, whereas everyone knows that I have no hope!" Fausto exclaimed, clapping his hands while his whole body rocked with laughter. Franco smiled and Fausto continued: "People have always said that about us, and this has never been truer than today." He stood up, went to the fridge and took out a bottle of prosecco. He examined the label and replaced it.

"Hold on for a minute." He left the room and raced down the stairs, returning with a bottle of champagne.

"This calls for a celebration," he said, popping the cork and pouring the effervescent liquid into the two flutes he'd magicked from a small wall cabinet.

"*Salute* to you and Nadezhda and to a long life together. Now, tell me, when is it going to be?"

"Well, I was thinking about the fifteenth of February, the day after Valentine's Day," Franco said, jiggling his hands in the air, shaking his head and hunching his shoulders. His gestures implied that the actual date itself was unimportant; after all, according to his diary, the year ahead was almost completely free, so the wedding could take place at any time. "To tell you the truth, I hadn't given it much thought, but since a few people were pressurising me to make a decision, I thought – why not St Valentine's feast day? I soon discovered that since he's not the patron saint of any old marriage but only of happy marriages, that day has been booked for the next five years. I'm glad really, because it would be a bit corny to be married on his actual feast day. That's why I've gone for the fifteenth."

"Surely, you don't mean that? If you do, that's incredible because that's *my* name day!"

"San Fausto?" Franco was not quite sure whether his cousin was pulling his leg again.

"Typical of my mother to give birth on the feast day of Saint Faustino who, it has to be said, doesn't rank high in the Church's hierarchy of saints."

"Never heard of him. You're making him up. You really are a rogue," Franco said, pulling the olives towards him.

"I hadn't heard of him either until one day, at the beach, I was flicking through a newspaper colour supplement and an article dedicated to this virtually unknown saint caught my eye."

"That doesn't surprise me."

"What doesn't surprise you?"

"That you were at the beach reading a colour supplement and were instantly attracted to a piece about a saint with your name," Franco said, reaching over to give his cousin a nudge.

Fausto ignored the allusion to the demi-playboy image of him, one favoured by some of his fellow citizens, and continued: "The article was a real eye-opener. I learnt that there are hordes of Italians who are committed to singledom."

"Hordes? That many?"

"Oh, I don't know. Let's say a considerable number of people. Everyone exaggerates. Anyway, in this case, enough people have grown up and become so fed up having to exist in the shadow of St Valentine's big name-day celebrations that they decided to dig around in the Vatican mud to find a saint whose name day was as close as possible to February the fourteenth. It turned out that Saint Faustino's feast day is on the fifteenth. Now, since most single-interest, proselytising groups attract individuals who are fanatical and uncompromising in the promotion of their one idea, it will come as no surprise to you, my dear philosopher librarian cousin, that this particular group had its zealots."

"I know what you mean. So, what was it that this group of zealots began to champion and insist upon?"

"Elementary, my dear Franco. They decided to take their cause one step further and have the feast of Saint Faustino elevated to the status of, yes, Singles' Pride Day, which is pronounced as SPeeD."

"Really? I've never heard of it. What's the point? I mean, do they have a programme of events for singles for that day?" Franco asked, eager to know more.

"I repeat myself. Elementary, my dear Franco. It's an awareness day."

"Awareness of what?"

"What do you think?"

"Not the faintest idea."

"Well, first of all, it's about awareness of the status of being single and, secondly, awareness of the discrimination faced by people who are not married and who consciously choose to remain single. Personally speaking, I can't see the need to celebrate being single. I'm quite happy with my status but it's nothing for me to shout about and extol. As to the choice of date, well, I have my doubts about the logic behind it. Could easily be interpreted as a sign of the group's inferiority complex. However, I don't know about you, but I don't think that logic counts for much these days," Fausto almost whispered, his fingers spread wide open on the counter, like a card player displaying his hand.

"You're right there. Logic and reason, as we understand the words, refer to faculties that are in short supply," Franco the philosopher pronounced.

"On the other hand, I suppose that it's not such a bad idea for everyone to have a saint to watch over them. What do you think? Look, you've got Saint Francesco, one of the best in the Vatican's book, whereas my Saint Faustino has probably been relegated to the company of third-tier saints."

"Oh, don't exaggerate. I'm sure that he's the ideal guardian for you," Franco said, smiling.

"You're quite right, for the good news is that this scarcely known martyr came from a wealthy pagan family."

"Well, that says it all. Everyone who knows you would concede that your mother couldn't have chosen a better date to give birth to her much-cherished and only son who, she instinctively knew, would turn out to be the rascal that you are, and therefore need and deserve an appropriate church-approved protector."

Fausto topped up their glasses; they clinked, laughed and embraced. "Of course I'll be your best man. And what a perfect date for you to get married and have as an anniversary. If it ever happens to me, I think that I'll also choose that as my wedding day. It would please my mother – though that's not a fact that I would tell the bride, unless she asked me."

"I'm ever so sorry, Fausto, I forgot to ask. How is she?"

"Much the same. The nuns look after and pray for her. Costs a fortune. But what's money?"

★

Initially, the wedding was intended to be a small civil ceremony attended by a few close friends and relatives, not one of whom would have staked a single lire bet on Franco ever summoning the energy to cross the Rubicon into marriage. Because his announcement had been so unexpected, every member of the family regarded the act as nothing short of a miracle, none more so than his father. He was so overjoyed at his younger son's decision that, as family patriarch, he pronounced that the wedding was an occasion to be properly celebrated in a traditional manner.

Despite their collectively declared atheism, the family elected to hold the wedding in San Stefano Church, with Dom Filippo officiating. The number of guests on Franco's side had to be restricted since Nadja had few close friends and had lost contact with most of her relatives, apart from a few distant cousins in Puglia, two of whom made the journey. As both were female, when it came to choosing a man to give her away, she was faced with a limited choice and opted for Alessandro the insider, over Piero the outsider.

At the reception in the community hall that followed, Fausto treated the guests to a witty and waggish speech.

Besides giving an affectionate description of Franco's idiosyncracies, he pointed out that, despite appearing to be the most easy-going and carefree person imaginable, the bridegroom was in reality an exceptionally reflective, considerate and sympathetic individual. He also alluded to the fact that Franco had a nickname for Nadja, which he had only once, and then inadvertently, used for her in front of him. When guests called out demanding he reveal it, he politely and firmly declined the request. "I'm deeply sorry," he said, "but Franco, who I can assure you is not at all secretive, has strictly forbidden me to disclose this most affectionate and intimate of names to anyone."

He then referred to the date itself, the fifteenth of February, his name day when a man called Faustinus was martyred under the emperor Hadrian. "That was in the year 120, which is a rather long time ago. Since learning of his existence, I've had to live with a great sense of disappointment that he's the patron saint of Brescia up there in Lombardy rather than of one of our towns down here."

"Ah, yes, but we don't need to worry. We've got our own saint Fausto, don't we, Dom Filippo?" someone called out.

Fausto then joked about no-hopers, like himself, and pointed to the main entrance of the town hall, outside of which was standing a young woman wearing a bright yellow vest and holding up a placard proclaiming that it was 'Singles' Pride Day'. Everyone in the wedding party, other than those who suffered from stiff necks, turned their heads to look at the stock-still young woman.

"That's the sort of young person that I admire," Fausto said, with a serious expression. "She heard about the wedding and, knowing that it was to be on the fifteenth of February, felt that she had to come here to take a stand against prejudice and injustice." His serious look had turned into an angry frown. He hesitated and then, ever the man for timing, said: "When you stop to think for a moment, this is a very spirited thing to do. In fact, I think that she's very brave. Don't you?"

The guests, who had replaced their masks of comedy with those of tragedy, stopped staring at the young woman and turned back to look at Fausto, whose face gradually began to crease as his mouth opened into a smile. "Let me introduce you to Chiara. She's getting married next year and, as we all know – don't we, Franco? – weddings are expensive occasions." Fausto paused and grimaced. "Therefore, she seeks to boost her tiny income – and I do mean tiny, since she's in that most creative but precarious of professions, yes, she's a budding actress – by taking on all manner of casual jobs. This time, it's raising money for a charity that has come up with the brilliant idea of attracting attention and money by concocting hoaxes such as this one. Not bad, don't you think? Just the sort of prank that our old friend Piero, *il capitano* here, likes to play. Since she's staying on for the reception, and if you would like to find out more about her and the charity she's helping, you can catch up with her later." Fausto finished and bowed to his audience.

The sighs and groans, which had been the guests' immediate response to the young woman's placard, were suddenly replaced by an eruption of noisy clapping as Fausto's short-lived balloon of seriousness floated over their heads and deflated, compelling everyone in his theatre to revert back to wearing their masks of comedy. Fausto granted the nuptial congregation time to rollick in a way reminiscent of a Bruegel tableau of a post-harvest bucolic feast, then called them to order and recited a list of events recorded as having occurred over the centuries on the fifteenth of February.

"Did you know that on this day in 399 BC, the male-citizen jurors of Athens sentenced Socrates to death for impiety and for corrupting the minds of the city's youth? All I can say is this: take note, young Franchino, because not only Socrates but the two predecessors of the Byzantine emperor Justinian the Second were doomed to similar hapless ends." Fausto adopted the grim air of a condemning judge, his eyes touring the spectators in his coliseum.

"Come on, Fausto, what happened?" Antonio called out.

"He had them executed in the Hippodrome of Constantinople. Admittedly, that too was a long time ago, but, nevertheless, on the fifteenth of February. So, Franco, what would you prefer on the anniversary of your wedding: a cup of hemlock or a beheading in Piazza Garibaldi? I think that you'd all agree that while Piazza Garibaldi isn't quite as grand as the Hippodrome in Constantinople, it would be a good place for a public spectacle, though nothing as nasty as a beheading."

Amidst the boisterous chatter, Alessandro's voice

could be heard shouting out, "Yes, I could watch the whole thing from my window."

"What else happened on the fifteenth so that we know what Franco should look out for?" a young bearded man, a frequent user of the library, asked.

"All right. Here are two more people who were born on the fifteenth of February," Fausto said, brandishing a scroll with his notes. "What do you think of this one: Piero the Unfortunate. To give him his full name, Piero di Lorenzo de' Medici. Born on the fifteenth of February 1472. He was intended to succeed as head of the Medici family and become *de facto* ruler of the Florentine state."

"Why was he dubbed the Unfortunate'?" Dom Filippo asked.

"I'll tell you. He was unfortunate in two senses. Bear with me; I'm being very brief. Firstly, he was arrogant and, as biographers say, undisciplined. Secondly, he died from poisoning when he was just twenty-two years old. While I don't expect this to be the fate of our librarian, I think that our mayor ought to be cautious."

"Absolutely! Franco is quite safe, but his brother, Antonio, would be well advised to borrow the armour that I wear as *il capitano del populo*," Piero's voice boomed out. "I know all about poisoned chalices."

"And who is your last choice?" a woman asked.

"Well, I'm most happy to say it's the date on which in 1867, Johann Strauss's *Blue Danube* waltz had its premiere in Vienna." This was the cue for a small band to strike up, and Franco and Nadja were clapped onto the floor.

After the wedding, Franco and Nadja continued to live in their prenuptial flat until Franco's father died and his stepmother, already suffering from advanced dementia, moved into the same care home as Fausto's mother, adjacent to the ruined convent. By that time, Franco had negotiated an arrangement with his brother and sister allowing him and Nadja to move into their father's house. Not long after they had ensconced themselves in his old family home, Franco had the vague sensation that Aeolus had blown into their lives a conception that until now each had privately thought about but never discussed.

*

It was a week before Christmas, and Franco was in the library slowly going through a set of photographs donated by Alessandro Galgano. They were to form part of a permanent exhibition about Montelorenzo that the two of them had planned to house in an annexe to the library, whose acquisition and conversion to meet its new purpose had, like the library, been partly funded by the Montedison Foundation. At Alessandro's invitation, Costanza had come down for a few days to attend the opening ceremony and had popped in to offer a helping hand, should one be required. Because of a concatenation of obligations and more pleasurable social engagements, she had hesitated before accepting the invitation; however, she knew that her long association with the town and the library project meant that she had a moral obligation to attend.

Franco and Costanza chatted effortlessly, each of them sensing that the other was unusually animated. Costanza was the first to take the risk and break the thin glass barrier inhibiting them from emotionally undressing.

"Is there something that you want to tell me, Franco? I think there is."

"That's exactly what I feel about you," Franco said, walking around to her side of the table and sitting down next to her. He had learnt that when two people are about to divulge to one another intimate information about themselves, unknown to anyone else, then the midwife that assists a person's delivery of the yet unspoken is the very fact of being physically close.

"Well, you tell me your news first," said Costanza.

"Nadja's pregnant," he said nervously, as he wasn't sure whether this was knowledge he had the right to disclose without Nadja's presence. But, having shared *his* secret that he was going to become a father and believing that one confidence deserves another, he looked Costanza in the eye and asked: "So, what's your news?"

"Oh, nothing compared with yours, Franco. Tell me – when is it due?"

"She discovered that she was pregnant not long after we moved back here. That makes her twelve weeks. But we're keeping it quiet for a bit longer. You're the only person I've told."

"Thank you, Franco. I feel very privileged." In fact, Costanza had never fully come to terms with how aggrieved she had felt about the manner in which she had learnt about Franco's intention to get married. By making her privy to Nadja's pregnancy, Franco enabled her simultaneously to pardon him, feel better, refocus her lens on their relationship and share *her* secret with him. But before turning to her news, she said: "That's an interesting choice of words."

"Which words?"

"You said, 'not long after we moved back here'. It sounds as though you've come home."

"Yes, you're right. Observant as always. And it's true. I never really enjoyed living down there on the coast. Strange as it may seem, I feel much more that I'm in the world of the living up here. Yes, I'm definitely much more at home."

"Now there's a subject that we could talk about, but I'm afraid it's one that will have to wait for another day," Costanza said, shaking her head at the thought of the twists and turns their conversational meanderings could take. "So, back to Nadja. Is there any chance of my seeing her before I go back to Florence?" Costanza asked.

"No. Sorry. Unfortunately not. You said that you're leaving on Tuesday, didn't you? By a stroke of bad luck, my Eurydice's away on a course and doesn't return until Thursday, which means that besides her not being at the opening of the exhibition, you'll miss one another again."

"What a pity. This isn't the first time something's happened to prevent us from meeting up. In fact, do you know, we haven't seen one another since your wedding."

"That's right. I think we've cancelled four times."

"I thought so. But just hang on a minute. What did you call Nadja?" she asked, with a look of surprise.

"Oh, it's just my nickname for her. I call her Eurydice and she calls me Orpheus. It goes back to the very first time we met. No, that should be the second time. That's when, because she had missed her bus, I took her back to her office on my Guzzi. Before we left the bar, I explained to her that, unlike too many motorcyclists, I never turn my head to talk to the pillion rider. I then gave myself the nickname of Orpheus and I called her Eurydice. When we got to know one another better and realised that we had something special, I used to sing to her, which helped to cement my name and hers by association. After all, you can't have Orpheus without Eurydice."

"How wonderful! How romantic! But you, a mythical hero? Some hope!"

"She's that too."

"You're confusing me, Franco."

"Don't be confused, Costanza. Nadja really is *my* hope. You should know by now that when you visit me, you deposit any confusion that you might have about anything at my front door."

"I forgot, but never again. Nor your pet names. Hers must be the one that Fausto refused to reveal to anyone at your wedding. I fully agree with you. Some nicknames are best kept private and confidential. They are the ultimate redoubt of a couple's intimacy."

The chuckle that accompanied her final words quickly faded. Something had happened to eclipse the sun that had been shining from the moment that Franco had announced his news, foreshadowing a change in her mood, which only someone with a long experience of kinesics would have detected. When she picked up the reins to her thoughts, it was to say, "It's not like you to tempt fate by choosing mythical nicknames."

"That's quite right. I've never been one to test fate or rely on chance or take chances. That's why I prefer to see our relationship as being based on faith. Fate, in the way it's often used, such as in the phrase 'we were fated to meet' doesn't come into our frame of thinking."

"And how would you describe this faith?"

"We never look back. We have our own separate pasts but only a joint future. And it's that joint future that we have faith in."

Costanza, who had studied classics before switching to pharmacology, was not at all superstitious and was used to his occasional – always opportune – references to Hellenic mythology, aware of an impish element in his character. However, what he had just said, though playful in intent, made her apprehensive. It sparked in her the memory of how, for the Greeks, the balance between the good and the bad that a person would experience during their lifetime was determined at birth by the Fates, who were represented by three ruthless sisters. Once a person's thread of life had been spun and measured, their final fate was inevitable and eventually dispensed by the third sister, Atropos, who decided when and how a person was to die, with no right to appeal.

Costanza shook her head and ran her fingers through

her thick dark hair as if in doing so she could root out the ticks of cynicism and pessimism burrowing into her scalp. Her coping strategy for dealing with these invaders was to giggle and say: "I'm tickled by the thought of you as Orpheus and can picture you in a *chiton* strumming a lyre." Despite her attempt to make light of her thoughts, Franco saw in her charcoal eyes and face an undisguisable gloominess.

"Oh, come on. Don't take it too seriously. It's a joke between me and Nadja which I thought I'd share with you. No one else knows, apart from Fausto. But listen, before you tell me your news, there's one other thing that has just happened on which I'd like to hear your opinion."

"I'm all ears. Go on, tell me. I hope it doesn't involve any more Greek and Roman deities or any other of their minor immortals."

"No, it doesn't, though I wouldn't be surprised if you found one that fits the following situation. It's definitely the sort of enigma I fancy you'd enjoy decoding."

"All right, try me."

"When I was leaving home this morning, Nadja put her arms around me and said, 'Franco, I've done it.' I didn't have a clue what it was that she'd done. She pulled herself back, took my hands and said, 'I've thrown away my handbag.' Franco looked at Costanza and waited for her response.

"Nothing wrong or unusual to say goodbye to a handbag, either one you've had for ages or one you bought only two weeks ago. Like most women, I'd rather not count the number I've given away or disposed of some how or other."

"Ah, but this handbag is quite different. For a start, it has always been more than a normal tangible bag in which you put things. Basically, when Nadja made the decision to separate from her husband and leave the village, she took with her in her handbag – and these are her words – a few small personal effects that were signifiers of womanhood. You know, eye make-up, mirror and that sort of thing. Like you, she's had countless handbags. All right, that's a bit of an exaggeration but you know what I mean. This one, though, is unique for several reasons. To begin with, it's the only one she took with her when she left her husband."

"So, you think that what makes this particular handbag somehow unique is its association with the ending of her relationship?" Costanza asked, visibly perplexed. She remained to be convinced that the incident that Franco was recounting merited the status he was according it.

"Perhaps not, but what does, I think, are two things. One is that in her words, when she left her husband, she placed the main trauma of her life and her phobia inside one of the zipped-up sections inside the bag. That's what she once told me, though I don't remember the context when the subject came up. I didn't at the time, nor at any other time, ask her what she meant."

"I'm sorry, Franco, but I don't quite understand what she means," Costanza said softly, crinkling her nose, before asking, "So, what's the second thing, as you put it?"

"Well, the second thing which leaves me flummoxed

more than anything else is the fact that this handbag has never ever left her wardrobe."

"Really? Is that true? She never used it at all?"

"It's not just that she never used it; she never even took it out of the wardrobe. What's more, it wasn't tucked away or hidden. No, it was there every time she opened the wardrobe. She couldn't miss it because it hung from its strap on the inside of the door." Franco finished talking and, giving Costanza an intense eye-to-eye stare, squeezed her wrist, as if in doing so he would extract a response from her: not any response but a response that in some way acknowledged what he liked to call the uniqueness of Nadja's attitude and behaviour towards this accoutrement. His serious tenor and demeanour had the desired effect. Almost, though not totally.

"'What can I say other than that for Nadja, this handbag and its contents are intensely personal and, though a mystery to anyone else, they are deeply meaningful to her," Costanza said softly and rather blandly, without expressing any sense of astonishment. She was still wondering where Franco's story was leading.

"Yes, congratulations, Costanza. It's as simple as that. But there's something that I should add in order to complete the picture. When Nadja said, 'I've thrown away my handbag,' what she meant was that she had at last said goodbye to her hoard of painful memories dating back, quite literally, to the day she was born. Does that make sense?"

"I'm sorry to say, Franco, that I find what you have

just quoted her as saying difficult to understand. My recommendation is that the mystery of the handbag is best unravelled and resolved by someone with a lot of experience of similar behaviour," Costanza said, deliberately refraining from inserting the adjective 'odd'.

"Do you mean a psychoanalyst?" Franco asked.

"Or a therapist or counsellor. These days, there's one on nearly every street corner. No doubt, among those you decide to select from will be a few who would classify her behaviour as a typically Freudian act. But, please, don't ask me to explain how *they* would interpret her behaviour," Costanza said, her anxious grimace ripening in the atmosphere into a relaxed grin.

"I know what you mean. You can't even scratch your earlobe without a local sage declaring your action to be open to Freudian interpretation," Franco said, disappointed by Costanza's response to what he regarded as a pivotal moment in Nadja's life. He had assumed that this dramatic episode was one with which Costanza would have empathised. However, since she clearly did not, or chose not to, see in Nadja's actions any link to her own life, Franco concluded that the train on which he had been driver and fireman had reached a terminus, so that it was time to alight, cross the platform, board another train and begin a different journey. The hiatus encouraged them to stand up and change seats. "Now it's your turn to tell me your secret," he said, patting her hand, imperceptibly relieved to reverse the heart-to-heart.

"All right, here we go," Costanza began, clasping her hands and biting her lower lip. "Almost exactly four months ago, I was introduced to someone. Since then, we've met up quite a few times. We went to a new exhibition together and then he invited me to a book launch and reception. After that, he came to a housewarming party thrown by one of my closest friends. It's been years since I've had such a hectic and exciting social life. Because we so often come up with the same ideas and hold identical opinions on a wide range of topics, we really feel that we are on the same wavelength. As a result, last week I revealed to him things about myself that no one else knows."

"Unknown even to Fausto or me?"

"No, not even to you or him. I've no idea why I did, but I did," Costanza said, looking over Franco's shoulder towards the library entrance.

"And?" Franco prompted.

"What you said a minute ago, about Nadja and her handbag, is making me think. I suppose that by confiding in him painful memories, some dating back to when I was a teenager, I was doing something similar to what Nadja did."

"Quite possibly," Franco said, her words reviving his dampened spirit as the chilly mist that had encased them began to lift.

"But I don't think that I'd ever go as far as she did. All those tangibles and intangibles that she had packed away in what she calls her handbag – they were all integral to her as a person. To disclose, as I did, is not the same as to dispose. Neither she nor I can get rid of our painful memories and traumas altogether. And, what's more, take it from me, no one but no one, if they're being truthful, ever reveals everything about themselves, and most definitely not every little thought they've ever had. Most human beings, now and again, think things, imagine things, dream things and wish for things which aren't nice. In fact, these things which we think or imagine can vary from the nasty and unpleasant to the dreadful and horrendous. They can be, literally, the unthinkable. It's precisely because these are thoughts we wish we didn't have that we keep them private; they're our personal secrets and we don't reveal them to a single soul."

"True. Unless you're a good Catholic and confess your wicked and sinful thoughts to a black-frocked priest."

"Or, if you're not, then you have the option of pouring out those same sickening thoughts to a white-coated secular confessor to whom you pay a substantial fee for the privilege of relieving yourself of a heavy mental burden. Is it a price worth paying?"

"Catharsis, Costanza, catharsis," Franco said, shaking his head.

"No more catharsis for me, Franco. You'll be suggesting abreaction therapy next. But look, as far as Nadja's dumping of her handbag is concerned, in my opinion, you should be pleased that she feels happy. Taken at its face value, what she's saying is this: something which has been weighing her down for years has been removed. As a result, she feels more at peace with herself. As far as I can understand, she's not told you what that burden was and why and how it has been removed. So, my advice to you is: smile with her and for her. Based on what I know of her, I can't help but think that she's on a journey."

"Aren't we all?"

"Of course, yet the obstacles and difficulties, and also, of course, the delights we confront on our individual journeys vary tremendously. Just think of the people we know as friends, acquaintances and neighbours. Not to mention relatives. Some journeys turn out to be full of hazards, unwanted and unsought, while the journeys of others are, conversely, equally hazardous but as a result of deliberately taken risks. At the other extreme, we both know individuals whose journeys seem to be perfectly tranquil, with only sporadic minor upsets, like passing clouds in otherwise totally blue skies. Funnily enough, the person I'm thinking of, whose life was like that, used to moan and groan about her existence as being excruciatingly boring, monotonous and tedious, which left her envious of people whose lives were dominated by unremitting emotional pain and suffering. Listing and describing types of journey would make a good party game," Costanza said, with a wistful half-smile.

"One probably already exists."

"That's true, but let's stay focused on Nadja. Without wanting in any way to pre-empt the diagnoses that therapists or psychoanalysts might come up with, I'd say that she's reached an important stage in her life's journey and told you so. Personally, I don't think you need to fret about the intention that lies behind her telling you what she has done. Accept that it's a symbolic act and probe no further."

"I reckon that what you've just said is your way of warning me not to open Pandora's box."

"You said it. Now, come on, let's fix a time and place to meet for supper."

After they had agreed a date and settled on Il Cinghiale Bianco, they both stood up and Franco put his arm around Costanza's shoulder, cleared his throat and gave a rendering of an aria from Offenbach's much-appreciated operetta. When he had finished, Costanza hugged him and, wagging her finger as if to a naughty child, said, "It won't be the first time I've told you that you have a beautiful voice. That's probably why Nadja married you. Well, not the only reason. I'm joking."

"Thanks for the compliment. It's not the first time that you've praised my singing and it's not the first time that I've said that you're too complimentary, especially in this case. But that's enough about me. I don't know whether you've noticed what a marvellous sense of humour Nadja has."

"I'd call it sharp and subtle, or subtly sharp." Costanza's quip expressed her own ambivalence on this aspect of Nadja's personality, whom she felt definitely inclined towards earnest on a rating scale from serious to playful. However, she had made up her mind not to undermine or contradict the image that Franco had generated of the person who was now his life-long companion and mother-to-be of their unborn child.

"When I said 'sense of humour', what I really meant was that she appreciates a humorous twist to reports of the misdoings and misadventures of our elites. She also likes to have fun now and again," Franco said, adjusting his interpretation of what Nadja found amusing to correspond more closely to Costanza's view of her. "It's in order to celebrate her fun-loving aspect that, when it's all over – if you know what I mean – I'm going to encourage her to take part in… Guess what."

"I haven't a clue," Costanza answered theatrically, by opening her eyes wide in childlike expectation.

"A performance of the same Offenbach operetta that I've just serenaded you from."

"What! Really?" Costanza exclaimed. "You have to put some pieces together, because I'm a bit lost again."

"Yes, I'm sorry. Here's a bit of background, which will probably surprise you. Nadja has been a member of Fortecantina's operatic society for over a year, which is related to the first time we met Piero together. That was when I learnt that, although she likes opera, she prefers those that are amusing and entertaining. This makes Offenbach's comic opera, which lampoons the Orpheus myth, a perfect choice for her. To top it all, according to the Society's programme, it's scheduled to be performed at the end of next year."

When he finished describing his vision of one particular, extended moment in their future, Costanza detected in his mile-wide smile and wide-open eyes the external manifestation of an inner calm and perfect contentedness. Feeling herself drifting under Franco's aura of tranquility, she said with an exuberant laugh, "I trust you don't envisage a part for her in the can-can chorus, because she won't be up to kicking her legs like that for a while." At that moment, an ebulliant Alessandro Galgano came through the door.

"You couldn't have come at a better time, Alessandro," Franco shouted out to him. "I was hoping to bump into you today."

His arrival coincided with Costanza glancing at her watch and gasping, "I'm so sorry, Alessandro, please don't think me rude, but I have to rush off. I've an appointment with the estate agent in fifteen minutes. In any case, there must be masses of things for the two of you to talk about before the opening."

"What am I supposed to have done wrong now?" Alessandro asked, pursing his lips and jutting out his jaw.

"Why are you always so paranoid?" Costanza asked, picking up her handbag.

"I'm not always. Only sometimes. And, when I am, it's usually with good reason," he replied, waving his rolled-up newspaper at Costanza while turning his head to wink at Franco. "What was it that you wanted to see me about, young Franchino? Nothing to do with the exhibition, surely. I thought that we had everything organised down to the last embroidered stitch."

"No, no. You're quite right. We've sorted everything, so there's nothing more to do. I wanted a word with you about an altogether different matter. I know it's a long shot, but I wondered whether someone or other in one of your social networks might have the name of a good gynaecologist."

"Yes, as it happens, I do," Alessandro said, puffing out

his chest. "By pure coincidence, it's someone in one of the best social networks in Italy; my cousin in Genoa. As you can imagine, he has friends who are gynaecologists. Better still, he himself has a first-rate reputation as being one of them." Alessandro paused, cocked his head and asked: "For Nadja, is it? Don't tell me! She's pregnant? No, no, you don't have to answer. Let me just say that, unlike so many eminent gynaecologists, my cousin is, just like me, not at all pompous. I'll put you in touch with him."

"Your cousin? A gynaecologist? Really! I'm glad I asked. And the icing on the cake is to know that he's exactly like you," Franco said, without a blink.

"I know that I thanked you quite a while ago for the sound advice you gave me on how to deal with that acned gigolo Lombardi. It would have been a total disaster for me if the *comune* had closed my campsite. But I never really thanked you to the extent that I should have. Now, perhaps, I can repay you properly."

At this point, Costanza stood up and with just a trace of a moistening eye gave Franco a hug and a kiss. As she walked towards the door, she turned back to him and said softly with an ethereal smile: "Social contacts, friendships? See you at Il Cinghiale Bianco."

★

It was a Sunday in the last week of May when they sat down to lunch. The restaurant was crowded because, when they had booked, they hadn't realised that it was Ascension Day, nominally the highest-ranking feast day in the Roman Catholic Church. Although not a public holiday in Italy, as it is in Austria, France and Germany, they regretted not choosing another date, which they could easily have done.

Nadja was noticeably big and her face quite pale, paler than usual; it certainly lacked the rosy glow of late pregnancy. The four diners, two of them old friends, wanted to get on well together, and they did: Franco and Costanza were the toastmaster and ringmistress respectively. Costanza introduced Franco as her surrogate brother, which helped Nadja to bond with the new man in Costanza's life. Sadly, their collective threesome jollity was tempered by their reading of Nadja's facial expressions, which could not conceal the fact that she was in almost constant pain. What they could not know was the degree of pain. They silently hoped that her discomfort was what any woman would experience at six weeks from the predicted parturition date. At Nadja's insistence, they ordered dessert and cheese, which they ate faster than they would normally have done so that she could be taken home.

Nadja went straight to bed with pain in every part of her body, but the aching limbs and difficulty in breathing were as nothing compared to the burning in her abdomen. For a while, she managed to stem her tears since she didn't want Franco to feel any blame for the fact that she felt so ill. Only she could give birth – this was something she couldn't share with him. Over the next couple of hours, she began to grow more anxious about what was happening to her body. As the pain intensified, anxiety turned to fear and then to terror.

She told Franco that she wanted to be sick. He asked her if she would like him to take her to the bathroom; she said that she would prefer to stay in bed, so he brought her a bucket. She was violently sick, and traces of blood coloured the yellow vomit. She had a high temperature. Franco called the doctor. He soon arrived, examined her and made an emergency call to the hospital. The doctor was as familiar as anyone with the road from Montelorenzo to the main regional hospital, the distance and the journey time, yet he was convinced that they should wait for the ambulance.

The midwife, who was in the ambulance when it arrived, acted as usher for moving Nadja from her bed into the vehicle. The siren wailed and the blue lights flashed all the way down the hill, alerting any car or stray tractor to pull over. When they reached the main road – the one that ran straight for two kilometres – the driver put his foot down on the accelerator. He could see the rear lights of two vehicles ahead of him and the headlights of a single vehicle coming towards them and, in the far distance behind it, a single bright, bobbing light.

The ambulance co-driver turned on the siren again and the driver pulled out and overtook the first car and then, with his indicator blinking, moved to overtake the second, a slow-moving truck. At that moment, the bobbing light of a motorcycle travelling at a racing speed swerved out from behind the car in front of it, making a head-on collision with the ambulance seem unavoidable. By breaking hard, the ambulance driver enabled the motorcyclist to manoeuvre out of danger and speed away.

However, in doing so, the ambulance went into a skid, spun full circle in the road, was hit by the car that it had overtaken and ended up crashing into a telegraph pole.

At the inquest into Nadja's death, the coroner recorded that, according to the medical report he'd received and read carefully, had she reached the hospital, her life might have been saved. No one else involved in the crash died, not even the unborn child, who was delivered at the scene.

POSTSCRIPT

That was a long time ago. The barber's pole has long since disappeared and the Galgano campsite is now owned by a German company. The ramparts, parapets and the castle keep have ceased to grow and are now respectably wreathed with ivy, bramble, wild roses and a few stunted fig trees. Although, after the accident, Franco never again took his Guzzi out of the garage, his grown-up son, Carlo Tomaso, uses it to go to the beach when he comes to stay with him during the summer.

Like Nadja's father, Franco never remarried and has always lived alone. Behind his bedroom door hangs a small, bright-red patent leather handbag to which has been fastened an enamel broach imprinted with a Toulouse-Lautrec painting of the Moulin Rouge. The bag almost has the status of a sacred relic – one that serves as both his *memento vivere* and *memento mori*. And when he hums, sings or whistles, it is no longer Verdi's *La donna è mobile* but Gluck's *Che farò senza Eurydice.* When I recently visited Montelorenzo – the first time in many years – I bumped into the head of the district carabinieri who, over *un caffè,* assured me that, although the motorcyclist responsible for the accident has never come forward or been identified, the case remains open.

This book is printed on paper from sustainable sources managed under the Forest Stewardship Council (FSC) scheme.

It has been printed in the UK to reduce transportation miles and their impact upon the environment.

For every new title that Troubador publishes, we plant a tree to offset CO_2, partnering with the More Trees scheme.

For more about how Troubador offsets its environmental impact, see www.troubador.co.uk/sustainability-and-community